Halfway There

Meagan Auer

Contents

Chapter 1

I was sitting in English class on the verge of ripping off my ears and pulling my eyes out. Mr. Green's voice was so dry and annoying it would cause the most cheery person to become a downer. Although I had only been in this class for twenty minutes it felt like a whole school day. His class had the ability to just ruin an entire day that was full of laughter and joy.

I had one friend in this class and she was out sick today. Come to think of it Lizy always got sick right before this class and went home. She would show up in the morning, stay for first-third period after our free period she was gone. Always. No one ever says anything though. I was seriously considering disappearing before this class myself.

I found myself staring out the window looking at the snow fall from the sky and gently land on the ground. Michigan weather was beyond annoying. One second it was hot then warm then it became freezing cold. This explains why I had a jacket, hoodie, and winter coat all in the trunk of my car.

"Stacie...Stacie.....STACIE"

My mind was wondering off to all kind of places until I heard Mr. Green calling my name. I snapped out of my thoughts and by then the whole class was staring at me with amused facial expressions. I wanted to be anywhere but here right now.

"Yes Mr. Green" I said to him in an annoyed, sarcastic tone.

He gave me a stern look as I scooted down in my chair knowing he was going to give me yet another lecture on paying attention in his class and how I need this class to graduate.

He started "Stacie you really need to start paying attention-" but I cut him off.

"Mr. Green I've heard this speech five times since I've gotten in this class...I don't need it again. I need to listen...pay attention...because I need this to graduate" I mocked him, waving my hands around the way he would do.

"I get it...moving on." I added. I really just wasn't in the mood today and I was like ninety percent sure my little display of attitude would get me detention.

I knew exactly what he was doing when he went to his desk and went in the first draw on the left. I had seen him go to that side at least two times a week and I was the cause each time. I slowly gathered my notebook along with my cream colored shoulder bag and went to his desk to receive my wonderful detention slip but I couldn't leave without a smart remark.

"Mr. Green how am I supposed to pass this class if you always send me to detention?" I joked and went on by changing my voice into a whiny one and saying,

"I NEED THIS CLASS TO GRADUATE." He rolled his eyes in irritation and handed me my slip then pointed towards the door, never making eye contact with me.

When I arrived in detention my usual spot was always open. A small desk that was in a corner over by a window. I know...I have a thing for windows. They help me focus on my drawings and all my poems and stuff. I mean let's face it I didn't really fit in anywhere. My only friends were Liz and my notebook. The only reason I had Liz was because we grew up together.

We all know how easy it is to make friends when you're little. When in high school, the cliques matter, your clothes matter, your looks matter, and here at this school if you didn't have money, you really didn't matter.

I wasn't ugly. I was the awkward kind of cute as all my cousins would say. I didn't exactly take that as a compliment. Sure I had big bluish, grey eyes and my blonde hair was long and pink on the ends but that didn't make me awkward. Did it?

I had reached my seat and was lost in my thoughts by the time I finally looked around the detention room. I scanned the room and it was full of usuals (like me), up until I ran my eyes past this boy I had never seen before.

He had hazel eyes and brown hair that was cut short but his outfit is what caught my attention. He didn't have on any color. The brightest color on him was his eyes. He had on grey pants with a black jacket to cover up his black shirt and black shoes. He simply just looked angry and he was staring at me stare at him.

He was only two seats away from me and he was staring at me like I couldn't see him. I rolled my eyes and looked down at my nails. Out the corner of my eye I looked his way, he was still staring at me.

"Can I help you?" I asked him rudely

A smiled tugged at his lips like I amused him. A small dimple appeared in his left cheek and I think I began to blush because I was sort of checking him out.

"No, it's just your hair interests me." When he opened his mouth and spoke a deep voice filled the room and took me by surprise. I don't know if I expected his voice to be smaller or something but it shocked me.

I felt my cheeks heat up even more, I'm sure I was sitting in detention looking like a tomato and I couldn't control it.

"Umm is that a good thing?" I asked almost shyly.

He laughed, "Sure." he shrugged calmly. And went back to writing in his notebook.

My eyes widened in shock. He just went back to what he was doing like he didn't just talk to me.

"That's it? That's honestly why you were staring at me so long? Come on now." I asked, truly curious.

He looked up and ran his hands thru his short brown hair. His expression was blank and all he said was "Yup." popping the P.

I was confused but I just didn't push the situation. I didn't have the energy.

Chapter 2

After detention was dismissed I rushed out of the old rusty classroom and went to my locker to retrieve my coat. As I put on my grey trench coat and tied the belt around my waist I felt a hand drag across my lower back and send shivers up my spine.

I twisted my head around to find out where it came from but whoever it was must have quickly blended into the crown of moving teens. All of them yelling their highs and lows of the day while others were gathering their things like me.

I shrugged it off. It was probably just a mistake. I joined the crowd of teens that were heading for the parking lot. Ready to go home after such a long day, I pushed pass all the people who were just wasting time in the halls. It was the end of the day, go home, I thought.

When I got to the front door of our high school the cold winter breeze hit my face and I felt my pale nose turn red and my cheeks flush with unnatural color. I pulled on my hood as my teeth began to chatter. I really hated the winter time.

I ran to my clean black jeep and rolled my eyes because I knew it wouldn't be clean after the storm that was supposed to come tonight. I climbed into the jeep and threw my bag into the back seat. I sucked in a deep breath and took in the fresh scent of new car.

My dad had just brought me this car because he allowed my cousin to crash my other one at our last family reunion. Laughing at the thought and I started the car.

The drive home was long. About a 30 minute drive away from the school and a 45 minute drive if you were going into town.

On my home I sing along to the radio and moved my head to the music. People laughed at me when I pulled up to red lights but I didn't really care, I sing along anyway.

I pulled up to our gated community and let the gate controller know I was here. After he opened the gate I drove up the street to my home.

I parked the car and jumped out. Once again the cold air hit my face and I suddenly missed being in the heated car. I snuggled closer into my coat and found my way up the rocky walk way that lead to our huge wooden door.

I opened the door and stared around the foyer. The silver spiral stair case looked like it had just been cleaned and the house smelled of cleaning products and fresh flowers.

"Dad" I shouted as loud as I could.

Silence filled the house and I rolled my eyes because I knew he was probably out or at work.

We weren't poor. Far from it actually but I chose not to flash it like everyone else did at my school. Only one who knew how well off I was Lizy.

Speaking of Lizy, I wonder where she was. As I found my way up the stairs I pulled my phone out of my back pocket and dialed Lizy's number. It rung a few times before she answered in a cheerful voice.

"Sup?" She shouted.

"First, why are you yelling? Second, why the hell do you always leave me in Mr. Green's class alone? Third, where the hell do you go?" I asked playfully as I walked the long narrow hallway to my room.

Liz laughed loudly into the phone and said "You should really keep up Stac; All you have to do is walk out..."

"Well sorry I'm not used to just strolling out of school like you are." I joked as I entered my room.

I sat my bag down by the door and kicked off my shoes, letting my sock covered feet sink into the cream colored carpet. Lizy was now going on and on about something or some guy. I wasn't really paying attention.

My stomach growled so I made my way back downstairs to the kitchen.

The coldness of the kitchen's tile floor made my warm feet curl up. The emerald green marble counters shined like they had been freshly glossed and the white kitchen appliances' stood out against the hard wood cabinets.

"Hey, Liz...I'll call you back. Kay?" I said

"Kay, Kay." she shouted cheerfully on the other end and hung up.

I hung up the phone and slipped it into the back pocket of my skinny jeans. I walked over to the refrigerator and opened it up. EMPTY.

My dad needed to seriously start at least stocking this thing, or hiring someone to do it for him since he always forgot.

I shrugged off the fact we didn't have any food and just ran upstairs to grab my bag and put on my coat and left. I figured I could just go down to the cafe nearby and pick up something to eat there.

When I got to the cafe, I took a seat in the corner where I always sat when I came here. The black barstools and sliver tables always made the cafe feel like it belonged in outer space.

I ordered a chicken salad and as I waited I began to write in my journal. I scanned over the cafe and my eyes stopped when they met a pair of greyish, hazel eyes that were staring directly into mine.

I tried to break our stares but I couldn't. His eyes were what really caught my attention. They drew me in and I was staring at him. A smiled tugged at his face and dimples appeared on his cheeks.

"Hi." he stated causally.

I meant to speak back, but instead I just kept staring. Maybe surprised that he had really just spoken to me.

Chapter 3

"Hi." he stated causally.

I meant to speak back, but instead I just kept staring. Maybe surprised that he had really just spoke to me.

"Me?" I asked innocently pointing to myself. I wanted to place my palm over my forehead and say "Real smooth Stacie. Real smooth" but I didn't need to appear as a bigger dork than I already did.

He laughed, showing more of his perfect white teeth and his dimples got deeper. "Yes, you." His voice was deep, yet so gentle.

I felt myself blush and I had to resist the want to smack my hands over them to cover it. I wasn't even the blushing type but Lord knows I had been doing it a lot today.

A big smile tugged at my lips "Oh, I knew that." I joked nervously. "Hi." I said moving a strand of hair from my face and tucking it behind my ear.

His eyes followed my movements and I shifted timidly in my chair. His gaze moved to my hair and I knew it was coming. The questions. Why pink?

"What?" I asked as he stared at me. What was up was there something on my face that I didn't know about cause everyone seemed to keep staring at me today.

"Nothing, your hair is just..." he paused as if he was looking for the right words to say that wouldn't offend me. "Different" he smiled after he found the correct word.

I smirked. "So I've been told." turning back to my notebook and picking up my pen.

"I didn't mean it in a bad way." he pointed out. His voice was apologetic, but truthfully he hadn't offended me at all. I was actually kind of flattered.

I turned his way again and moved my hair once more, slowly becoming annoyed with it now. "You didn't offend me." I smiled. "Thank you."

His face lit up again but died quickly when the waitress brought me my food in a to go bag.

I smiled and handed her a tip and stood to gather my things.

"Nice meeting you...." I started but couldn't finish when I realized I didn't know his name.

He stood himself and extended his hand, "Isaiah." he smiled.

When he stood he towered over me. I was only 5'2; he had to be about 6 feet. His body was slim and his tight white shirt showed off his body underneath. I took his hand

and wrapped my own around it firmly, giving a sweet smile. "Stacie."

He gathered his things as well and that is when I noticed he had already had his food and didn't really have a reason to still be here. I smiled at the thought that maybe he stayed here just to talk to me. I blushed again.

He walked away before me and exited the cafe without any more words. When he walked away I opened my hand and found a small piece of paper.

I could still feel the warmth of his larger hands on mine as I opened up the piece of paper he slipped to me and read it.

554-8914. I couldn't control the smile that welcomed itself on my face and looked up to see if anyone else had noticed my foolish school girl smile.

My alarm went off and I had the sudden desire to throw it across my large bedroom. But that would mess up the mint green paint on my walls and destroy the art work that was mounted so I decided not to.

I turned off the alarm and dragged my barely alive body to the bathroom up the hall since the one in my room had a broken shower. Long story.

I brushed my teeth, washed my face, and showered, all within 30 minutes. Now, getting dressed is what would take forever. No, I wasn't the type who was all over dramatic about my appearance but I didn't leave the house looking any kind of way.

I stood in the middle of my walk-in closet and I couldn't find anything that I wanted to wear. My shoes were neatly lined up on the shelves, by color. My converse collection neatly on one shelf, going from lightest to darkest. Those were my babies.

Heels and flats, I didn't care much about those but were in color order too. My boots, those were like my pets seeing as though I wear boots year around.

I grabbed my black combat boots with the buckles and matched it with a simple graphic tee and cut up white skinny jeans.

I pulled my long hair up into a messy bun, letting some strands fall if they wanted because I was too lazy to fix it. I applied a little black eyeliner, grabbed my bag and headed off for school.

When I got there I was a little early so I found my way to my locker. It was dirty and seriously needed a cleaning out. Right when I was on my way to do so, my iPhone buzzed in my back pocket.

I knew it wasn't anyone but Liz but I pulled it out to check the text message anyway. I figured since no one was really at the school yet I could walk and text at the same time. Mistake.

As I was texting my body crashed into a tall, firm figure and threw me off balance. His strong arms caught a hold to my wrist before I fell. I began to mutter a sorry and move hair out my face that fell out of my already messy bun.

"Stacie?" his voice asked with question.

I looked up and met his eyes, the same greyish, hazel eyes from the cafe. I couldn't help but smile and blush because I hadn't even had a chance to Text the guy yet and I had already displayed my clumsiness.

The last place I expected to see him was here. Sure he was cute, beyond cute actually but he didn't look my age.

He was still holding onto my wrist gently and I was beginning to feel the warmth of his hands all over again. His touch tickled and I liked it.

"What are you doing here?" I asked

He smiled "I work here." he said like I was supposed to know that.

My eyes widened in shock and I felt the need to take my wrist from his hands. So that's exactly what I did. Confusion filled his face.

"Wait, what are you doing here?" he asked

"I go here silly." I said casually.

People were beginning to pour into the building. Isaiah and I didn't move though. Our bodies were a little close so I took it upon myself to move back a few inches.

His face was now a pale white and he looked disappointed. "Umm, I have a planning period. And

I nodded my head but I didn't say anything else. He walked away from me and pushed his way through the small hallways of the high school.

I felt like a little bit of hope had just died in me. I had been so excited when I left the cafe yesterday, but any chance I had of getting to know him had just been ruined. I couldn't date him now.

A small hand touched my back and I knew instantly it was Lizy.

"I was gonna go off on you for not responding to my text, but now I see why you didn't" she joked. I'm guessing she'd seen Isaiah.

Lizy had big brown eyes and chocolate brown long hair. She sort of reminded me of a bunny. She hopped around and was always cheerful. I always wanted to grab her cheeks. Although now, I really didn't feel like dealing with her cheerfulness when my dreams had just been ruined.

When I just start walking towards my locker, she'd followed my lead and started walking with me.

"Who was that?" she asked "He's hot" she added excited.

"You know I'm not sure of his last name." I looked at her, but I was actually just making a statement to myself. Not exactly talking to Lizy.

"Then what's his first name." she beamed

"His name is Isaiah." I said while opening up my locker and letting out a big sigh.

Chapter 4

"Stacie..." Lizy sharp elbow crashed into the side of my stomach.

I gave her a death glare and rolled my eyes at her. She has been doing the shit to me for the last three periods. "Will you stop that?" I whispered through clenched teeth.

She put her hands up as if she surrendered. "Fine." she said and turned her head back towards the board.

We had been sitting in Chemistry class for the last twenty minutes and it was beginning to become torture. Today I regretted picking Lizy as my partner because she was really getting on my nerves. She kept asking how I knew his name was Isaiah if he just started working here.

Clearly if I didn't answer the first four times I wasn't going to answer, but Liz didn't get that. Plus my legs were starting to get numb from sitting on these old wooden bar stools.

The chem lab was a little too small for my liking. Only because it was thirty students in here, and the class could barely fit twenty. There was fifteen little steel tables, each one having two barstools. Only one mircoscope at each table.

Our chem teacher was going on and on about something. Molecules in DNA or something like that. I wasn't really paying attention, I didn't really care.

In the middle of my thoughts my phone buzzed in my pocket. I pulled it out and checked my new text message.

Nice giving each teacher your cell phone number. -Isaiah.

I couldn't help the smile that took over my face. I knew Lizy was staring at me because she soon knocked her elbow into my stomach and whispered "What's got you smiling?" she smiled.

I wanted to yell at her for killing my left side but I knew that would draw too much attention. I couldn't even give her a mean look because I was still smiling at the text message. It was true; I'd given every teacher my cell phone number. The way I seen it if you wanted to call my house, at least call a phone that would really answer. No one was ever home.

I smiled at Liz but I didn't tell her why I was smiling.

"Is there something you guys would like to share?" Our teacher shouted

Lizy and I both looked up and stared at our teacher. Lizy put on a sweet smile and said "No." Me, I wasn't in the mood and I couldn't seem to bite back my sarcasm.

"Sure, I would." I smiled

Lizy once again tried to knock her elbow into my side but I grabbed her this time. She whispered, "Stop Stac." I only laughed and glared back at the teacher.

"Really Stacie. Go ahead." My teacher said with her own hint of sarcasm.

"There's makeup on your teeth." I smiled and some of the class began to laugh, including Lizy.

The teacher winced at my statement and ran her tongue over her teeth in horror.

She put her hand over her mouth and said "that's deten-tion."

I was already gathering my things before she even said I had detention. I whispered a goodbye to Liz, took my slip proudly and left. I had been plotting how to get out that class the whole twenty minutes I was in there. Just so happened I had to inform her about the makeup on her teeth to get out of there. That was tragic but her face was priceless.

When I got to detention I took my usual seat and pulled out my notebook.

"Fancy seeing you here." a familiar voice said from beside me.

I hadn't really looked around before I sat down and honestly I hadn't noticed anyone come sit beside me.

I looked up and my eyes met the same pair of hazel ones I'd seen last time I was in detention. He was so close. He was leaning on his arm and just staring at me. Like seriously did this guy have to confidence of super model or what?

I smiled coolly "Hi." I said and put my attention back to my notebook.

"What's your name?" he asked

"What's your name?" I replied instead of answering his question.

He laughed loudly before looking to see if the teacher noticed us talking. Not that Mr.Flownder cared; he didn't want to be here either.

He turned back to me and stared at me for a long moment. "You're cute." he pointed out.

I looked up to see his face to tell if he was serious. A smile was stretched across his face and his eyes were filled with humor. I rolled my eyes but I couldn't pass up a chance to put this asshole in his place.

"If that was supposed to make me blush, it didn't work." I said rudely

"Or did it?" he laughed once again.

I felt my irritation grow and I had officially decided I didn't like this guy.

"What's your name?" I asked again, hoping to change the subject.

"Carter." he grinned

"Well Carter, do me a favor. And please relocate to the other side of the classroom." I returned his grin.

He chuckled this time but he got up out his seat beside me, only to come in front of my seat and lean down in my face. Leaving our faces only inches apart and placing his finger under my chin, lifting my face forcing me to look into his beautiful eyes.

I sucked in my breath and my gaze dropped to his lips. He was smiling like he had somehow won.

"Nice meeting you Stacie." he whispered and let my face go.

Chapter 5

I had survived four days without detention but it was Friday and almost everything seemed to be moving slow. Except lunch of course.

Okay, I'm lying. I had only been at school long enough to get through my first period and I was currently on my way to my second. Art.

For once I was happy to have Liz in a class with me because I knew with my luck, the rumors about the new art teacher was true. Add on more of my bad luck, Isaiah would be that teacher.

I hadn't seen him since we bumped in the hall that one day and I haven't texted him since I got detention that other day. Come to think of it I hadn't seen him around at all. Like he fell off the face of earth or moved away and decided not to keep contact with anyone. I know, my imagination is wonderful.

"Are you even listening to me?" Liz said in an annoyed tone as we walked the halls together.

Honestly, I forgot she was beside me. I flashed her a puzzled look, "What were you talking about?" I said trying to give a sweet smile so she wouldn't yell at me.

"I was saying we should leave for lunch." she said while rolling her eyes at me. "You never listen anymore, you know that right?" she added

"Sorry, warn me next time you want to talk about something I don't care about." I said playfully.

"Shut up." she laughed.

We walked into our Art class laughing, not even really realizing we were late. The whole class turned their heads to look at us, a couple giving death glares like we had really interrupted something important.

My eyes slid over to the tall, familiar figure standing in the middle of the class. The class was set up in a circle, making it so we see everyone's face. No tables today, just the chairs. This sort of made it look like an AA meeting.

Isaiah standing directly in the middle of the circle and glaring at us just like the rest of the class. I put on the best smile I could and I knew I was blushing. Lizy on the other hand was drooling like she'd never seen a hot teacher before.

Truth be told, we probably haven't. Not at this school at least.

"Have a seat." he ordered, pointing to the two empty chairs positioned directly behind him. This gave us a beautiful view of his ass. That thought only made my blush deepen.

I was staring up until Liz pulled me by my purse and guided me to the seat. A few people laughed but those were guys.

The girls were too busy making fucked up Megan Fox faces, attempting to look sexy.

"Okay. Now since that is over, back to what I was saying." he paused and I heard the amusement in his voice. "I'm Mr. Smith. Clearly I'm the new art teacher and this is how the class will be set up for all of next week." he said while walking around the middle of the circle.

"Why?" Paul asked from a few seats down from me. Paul was the loner no one really talked to but everyone knew who he was.

Isaiah laughed, "Ah I knew that question would come from somebody." he said while walking over to a chair that was also part of the circle and sitting down.

"Mrs. Miller knew you guys." he pointed out. "I don't." he said while shrugging his shoulders.

"So you mean to tell me we're going to be sitting in this circle to get to know each other?" Some snobby little girl said, sitting over by the door. Her, I didn't know.

"Yup." he said popping the P. Making the statement come off a tad childish.

Some of the class groaned but me, I was staring. Ever since he sat down his eyes were boring directly into mine as he spoke. I noticed a couple glances our way but no one really said anything.

I didn't care regardless. Liz called herself trying to get my attention by shoving her combat boots into my leg but I only cussed and told her to "fuck off" never taking my eyes off Isaiah.

Those beautiful hazel eyes of his sprinkled with amusement before he glanced down at his palms like a little boy.

"Stacie." Lizy whispered "Just drool why don't you."

I looked over at her and gave her my full attention. "Silence. I was not drooling." I whispered back thru clenched teeth.

"Sure you weren't." A huge smile stretched across her face and her eyes danced with mocking joy.

"Shut up." I blushed

Clapping his hands to get everyone's attention, mostly me and Lizy's. "So what's everyone's favorite color?" He beamed. "I'll guess yours is pink."

I wasn't really listening, just looking around until I felt everyone's eyes on me.

"Me?" I asked puzzled and pointing at myself.

He chuckled, "yes, you."

I slid down lower in my chair and tried to give the best confident expression I could. "Umm what was the question?" I smiled sweetly

"Is your favorite color pink?" he asked again while shoving his hands in his pockets nervously.

I cocked my left brow and tilted my head to the side, "Why would you think my favorite color was pink?" I seriously wanted to know.

Everyone in the class looked at me like I was crazy and I couldn't understand why.

He laughed hard this time. Dimples appearing in his cheeks and a smile taking over his face. "I just assumed your hair and all." he said still laughing.

I smiled. "My hair is just creative expression; my favorite color is lime green." I paused "I just figured lime green would be a really loud color to put in my hair." I half joked. That was truthfully why my hair wasn't green on the ends; pink already drew too much attention.

"Nice to know." he said still smiling. "And what about everyone else? We'll start from her and go left."

This went on for the rest of the class.

Chapter 6

The weekend. I mentally celebrated on my way out the school. I had it all planned out. I was going to sleep Saturday, all day. And I was going to eat Sunday, all day. Wicked plans, I know right.

I meant to ask Liz to stay over since I knew my dad would be away at a business trip. My mom was out of the question because she had been up her new husband's ass for the past four months. Our big house got lonely when it was just me and honestly it scared me out at night.

I texted Lizy and told her to swing by with enough clothes for the weekend and bring snacks. But knowing her she would show up with no clothes and end up leaving in mine. Right when I was about to climb into my car someone was shouting my name in the distance.

I rolled my eyes because I knew the familiar voice. It was no one but Carter. He had stopped by my locker and as he would say "casually passing by" in other words, he touched my ass.

"Shove it Carter." I shouted back.

I heard him laugh but still he was coming my way. "Will you slow down?" He shouted.

I didn't know why he was still shouting, he was inches away from me now,, no need to shout.

"Why in the hell are you shouting? My ears work fine." I said rudely.

"I couldn't tell the way you ignored me calling your name." He said out of breathe and leaning up against my jeep.

"Either you stand up straight or when I move this thing you fall into the snow, cause its cold and I'm not about to stand out here and talk to a guy I don't even like." I said with the same rude attitude from before. Although he didn't even attempt to get out the way.

"Move Carter." I yelled.

"Fine." he said calmly and walking around to the passenger side and getting in.

I opened my door and threw my bags inside, careful not to ruin my stuff from art class because I had a project I needed to finish for the art show next week.

"What the hell are you doing?" I asked, attempting to control my temper. "Don't you have a car of your own and some other female to bother?"

He laughed and started rambling through all my CD's. "Sure I do, but unlike them you don't like me. Therefore it's more fun to mess with you." His eyes lit up when he spoke and he was smiling like a little boy.

"It's the weekend, go home. Watch some porn. Get out my car and leave me alone." I said after climbing into my car and settling in.

He didn't even flinch, he just sat there, still as ever and quiet as a mouse. As I waited for him to get out my car, I pulled my hair up until a messy bun and started my car. Since he wasn't going to get out, we could go for a ride.

I began to pull out of the space I was parked in and I drove out the school parking lot. Still he didn't say anything. Two could play his game.

The farther away from the school I got, the more nervous he looked.

"Where are we going Stacie?" I heard the panic in his voice but I didn't respond.

I sing along to the music like I did every time I drove. We pulled up to my gated community and I let the gate controller know I was here.

"Who lives out here?" He asked looking out the window and taking in the surroundings.

Still I didn't reply, I just turned down my music because I knew my neighbor, Mr. Turner hated my loud music right after he got home from work.

When I pulled up in my driveway, I just got out the car without saying a word to Carter. I walked up to the door and he was still sitting in my car like a fool. He was just staring at me like he didn't know what to do. I motioned for him to get out the car and he followed orders.

He walked up to me and began to ask a million questions.

"Whose house is this? What about my car at the school? Why did you just kidnap me?" He asked quickly.

I laughed at the last question, "I didn't kidnap you Carter, and you got into my car willingly, and then refused to get out." I pointed out.

He stared at me open the door to the house with my keys and I see it click in his head.

"This is your house?" His eyes were wide and he stared around the yard like it was too good to be true. Although everything was covered in snow.

I nodded my head and stepped into the house. "Why do you sound so surprised?" I questioned curiously.

He looked around like a kid in a candy store when he walked inside, "Oh look, it speaks." He joked. "I just always took you as a...I don't know."

My eyes widened, "I just met you, and how could you take me as anything?" I dropped my bag and pulled off my boots.

"You just didn't seem like a rich girl." he said taking off his shoes as well.

"I'm not." I said calmly. "My dad is rich, not me. I didn't work for this."

"See that kind of attitude is what made me think you would stay in a normal sized home, not this." He waved his hands around then looked directly at the staircase.

"Any who." I tried to lighten up the mood. "Hungry?"

He laughed, "You're cooking?" He rubbed his hands up against his black skinny jeans, "I'll past." He half joked.

"Come on, I'm not that bad." I laughed and walked towards the kitchen, feeling him follow behind me.

When his footsteps stopped I knew his mouth dropped and he was staring around the kitchen. I think everyone does that the first time they see it.

"Don't get drool on the floor smart guy." I joked, opening the refrigerator and staring at all the new food that was in there. A couple days ago, it was empty. I made a mental note to tease my father about it when he got home on Monday.

"Shut up." he said, sitting on one of the barstools and smiling at me.

It was weird; I had just met Carter, in detention at that. Sure he was a jerk but he had his moments. Plus he was attractive and currently sitting in my kitchen.

I pulled out stuff to make us sub sandwiches. "Ham or Turkey?" I asked with my back turned towards him.

"Turkey." I heard him picking up the fruit from the bowl and I bet he was playing with it.

"Put the fruit down." I said. "Other people have to eat that."

"From the looks of things, you're the only one ever here."

I stiffened at his words, he didn't know anything. I rolled my eyes and walked over to the counter in front of him with the turkey and ham in my hands. Along with other stuff to make a sandwich.

"My dad's away on a trip." I pointed out while pulling out a knife and slapping mayo on the bread.

"I don't like Mayo." He pointed out nicely

"Not your sandwich." I said seriously and continued putting the mayo on my sandwich.

"Aren't you supposed to tend to my need first?" He asked smiling.

"What's wrong with your hands?" I asked, returning his smile with one of my own.

"Fine, I'll make my own." He got up and walked around to me, grabbing things to make his sandwich. Towering over me because I was 5'2 without shoes and he had to be 5'10 or taller.

"So how are you gonna get back to your car?" I asked playfully.

He looked over at me, eyes wide. Realizing he had left his car at the school. "You're going to take me." He demanded

"I'm not leaving this house all weekend buddy." I laughed loudly, finishing making my sandwich and sitting down in the place where he just was.

"Then I'll just stay here until Monday." he shrugged.

"And you'll go to school with the same clothes on?" I laughed, taking a bite out of my sandwich.

"I said, I'll stay here. Which means, sleep here. Get a ride to school on Monday. Get in my car, go home. Skip school." He said like he was the smartest person in the world.

"Fine." I said taking another bite.

"Sooooo, I'm sleeping with you." He laughed, and came to sit next to me with his sandwich and taking a bite.

"Haha, cute." I fake laughed. "You see this house, guest room up the hall asshole." I smiled

"That'll work, but I suggest you lock your doors. I can get a little touchy at night." He joked.

Right when I was about to reply, Lizy's loud cheerful voice filled the house. "I'm hereeeeee and ready for a sleepover."

I had completely forgot about the text I sent her. "I'm the kitchen Liz." I shouted back.

She skipped happily into the kitchen but stopped when her eyes met Carter's.

"Ahh, Liz, Carter. Carter, Liz" I said pointed to each one when I said their names. "Liz, Carter's going to be crashing our sleepover." I said in my sweetest voice.

Chapter 7

"So you guys seriously don't hit each other with pillows in your bras?" Carter asked stubbornly.

We had been having a fight for the past half hour about what girls really did at sleepovers. Apparently, Liz and I were supposed to be in our under clothes by now, smacking each other with pillows and confessing our deep dark lesbian love.

I rolled my eyes at Carter's stupid comment and shifted my body towards Liz. We were sitting in the living area where the television was, trying to pick out a movie.

"I'm really sorry I'm putting you through this." I half joked. She knew by this, I meant Carter and his unfiltered mouth.

He had winked at her several times and attempted to grab her ass when she got up to answer the door for the pizza man.

She laughed at me and peeked around my shoulder at a distracted Carter. He was busy browsing through Netflix, and not paying any attention to us.

"It's okay. You're lucky he's cute or I would be mad." She laughed out loud and her brown eyes danced with amusement.

Shoving her playfully and standing up from the fort, pallet, blanket, pillow masterpiece we made on the floor. We laid pillows down and spread out blankets on the floor and that's where we were sitting. It gave us a better view of the large flat screen tv mounted on the wall.

They both looked up at me, Liz shrugged. Not caring where I was going. Carter began with the questions.

"And where are you going?" He half shouted.

"My room father, is that okay." I bit out sarcastically, but playful enough so he wouldn't take me seriously. I had warmed up to Carter, he seriously wasn't that bad. And I had to agree with Lizy...he was cute.

He smiled, showing his one dimple. "Can I come?"

I rolled my eyes and motioned for him to come along, stepping over pillows and pizza boxes as I left the living area. Liz hitting me with a small pillow and winking when Carter wasn't looking.

Flicking her off and trying to make my way upstairs to my room. Still in my clothes from school, I wanted to get comfortable.

"I imagined it differently." He said.

I started to ignore him but I couldn't help myself, "Ohh you've been imagining my room ah." I said in a horrible Australian accent. Making us both laugh.

"No, smart ass." He said after laughing, "I just pictured it being black and grey with red stripes on the wall, in the form of blood dripping." He said, picking up stuff from my dresser and looking it over before playing with my jewelry.

I snatched some of my rings out of his hands and placed them back in the proper spot before I said another word. "Like your room?" I tilted my head to the side and looked him directly in the eye.

A slow, wicked smile creeping on his face. He was really attractive. What, was I checking him out? Snap out of it Stacie...get it together.

"How did you know?" He joked, his voice deeper than usual.

Breaking our gaze and walking around him, towards my closet. Feeling him follow closely behind me. I turned around abruptly, making him crash into my chest. I felt fire travel through my body when they touched and I stepped back absentmindedly.

"Who said you could enter my closet?" I asked, my voice coming out weaker than I wanted.

"I did, now enter or I'll enter it alone." He smiled, looking around me but not at me.

I groaned but eventually opening the double doors to my closet and stepping inside. I walked quickly over to the section with the nightclothes and grabbed a big shirt and some plaid night pants.

Turning a little, my head over my shoulder and looking at Carter ramble through some of my clothes. He was taking stuff out and putting it back in the wrong spot, messing up my color system. Marching over and trying to get the clothes out his hand but he caught me before I could.

Holding my hand and pushing it down before grabbing my waist and pulling me closer to him. Pressing our bodies together, and dropping the clothes he once held.

My breathing picked up and I stared at his chest, since he was taller than me. Grabbing my chin and making me look at him. Licking his lips, which caused my gaze to drop to the full lips he licked so slowly. Oh my God, I was staring at his lips. His so kissable lips. What the hell was happening to me?

Searching for the little confidence I usually have. Anything that would help me get out of this situation. He titled his head and leaned down, making his way to my lips. Slowly. So slow. So damn slow.

Almost there. Really close. Inches apart. My phone began to vibrate in my back pocket. I smiled softly and cursed whoever the hell it was for interrupting. Moving out of Carter's hold and retrieving my phone.

Glancing at the name and butterflies stirred in my stomach. I knew a creepy smile crept on my face and I felt Carter staring at me in confusion. Or maybe it was frustration. I pushed the thoughts back and the sudden need I felt to kiss him was gone.

I rushed out of the closet and ran to the useless bathroom on the other side of my room. Useless because the shower was broken. Baby cousin visited last month of summer, long story. Hoping Carter wouldn't follow me. I locked myself in the bathroom and quickly answered the phone before he hung up.

"Isaiah, Hi." I said calmly, trying not to sound too cheerful.

"Stacie. How are you?" His deep voice boomed through my phone and I instantly smiled.

"I'm fine. What's up?" I asked, sort of out of breath from my little track star moment back there.

"Why does something have to be up?" He replied with playfulness laced in his voice.

"Well one, you're calling me at..." I paused and snatched the phone away from my ear to look at the time. "10:25 PM, on a Friday night. Second, you called me in the first place." I laughed.

"Am I not allowed to call you?" He said with a laugh of his own.

"Welllll...technically." I laughed again, a stupid smile plastered on my face.

"Oh yeah." He laughed stiffly. "Well, how about we say this is a school matter."

"Okay, I'll go along with that." I nodded my head, like he could see me. "What can I help you with Mr. Smith?" I joked

He laughed loudly, but it didn't bother me. "Are you free? Right now." He paused for a few seconds. "If it's not okay with your parents you leave the house this late, I understand."

I laughed at the nervousness in his voice and at the fact he thought my parents cared. It was 10 not 3:00 am. Even then, my dad probably wouldn't care. I questioned if I was free, because I had Carter in my closet and Lizy downstairs in my living room. I wasn't exactly free.

"Maybe, why?" I finally said.

"Can you meet me, down at the park by the Cafe' we met at?" He said shyly.

I took a few moments to answer because I didn't want to seem as eager as I felt. My heart was doing backflips in my chest and my smile was beginning to hurt. "Umm sure. I can do that. Meet you in 15 minutes." Hanging up before he could say anything more.

I was about to leave this sleepover to meet a guy.

Not just any guy.

My teacher.

Chapter 8

Rushing out the bathroom and past an impatient Carter then back into my closet. Sure, I was still in my school clothes. Isaiah had already seen those. Therefore I had to change. Yes, this is me being a teen.

"Uh, who was that?" Carter asked sort of calmly, sitting on my bed.

I needed to think quickly and come up with at least a reasonable lie. Carter didn't know me that well, I could lie to him easily. But Liz would be all over me like hot cakes. Hot cakes? Whatever. Whichever lie I told to Carter I had to tell the same one to Lizy so it had to be believable.

"My mom." Blurting out the first thing that came to my mind. I hadn't talked to my mom in weeks almost.

"I heard you say Mr. Smith Stacie." Shouting loudly enough so I could hear him and the irritation his voice was suddenly filled with.

"Uhh, she's recently married. That's her last name now. I was talking to her husband, my stepdad when I said that."

Good one, real good Stacie. I mentally patted myself on the back for that one.

"Oh okay." He sounded uncertain but he let the subject go. "Where ya going?"

Crap, didn't think about that. Think. Think. Think. "I have to go give my mom some stuff and pick up some stuff. I'll just be stepping out for a half hour, no longer." Scrabbling and trying to pull up the faded jeans I pulled from my closet.

"Okay. I'll go tell Liz." He was calling her Liz? They just met. "You sound kinda busy in there." I heard the amusement in his voice then hearing him close my bedroom door.

I pulled a plain long sleeve light blue shirt over my head and pulled my hair out of the messy bun it was in, letting it cascade down my back and around my shoulders. Not even bothering to run a brush through it or grab a bag. I figure I won't be long. It was late Isaiah couldn't want much. Right?

Sprinting down the stairs and out the door before I could run into Liz. She would be able to tell I was lying. Plus she knew my mom didn't marry a guy with the last name Smith.

It took about ten minutes to reach the Cafe' and an extra five too arrive at the park he mentioned. I couldn't help but feel bad. Rebellious almost. It felt nice. The small butterflies in my stomach or the weird feeling like I was breaking the law. Well, I kind of was. But last time I checked there was no law against meeting an older guy at the park. Although, I had never kept up with the law.

My mind was going a mile a minute when I was walking over to Isaiah, who was childishly sitting on a swing instead of the park bench that wasn't far from him.

His back towards me. His messy hair seemed worse than usual. A white t-shirt that clung to his chest gracefully, his jeans. I couldn't tell. He was sitting after all.

"Having fun?" I sounded more playful than expected.

Peeking his head over his shoulders and glaring at me before letting his perfect grin enter my sight. "Very much." He nodded his head, motioning for me to fill the empty swing next to him.

I sat next to him and began to swing slowly. High but not that high. While I was swinging he didn't speak, only staring up at me with some unreadable expression.

Slowing my swing down to a stop, smiling over at him. Sort of feeling childish for just swinging in front of him. But I couldn't resist it, and hey...he was the one sitting on the swings first. I bet he was swinging just like me before I got here, I thought silently.

"Wanna tell me why I'm here?" I asked after he didn't speak.

He clapped his hands together, drawing my gaze to him before he spoke. "Why didn't you tell me you were in high school?" He sounded serious but I could still see the amusement in his eyes from before.

"Well, Mr. Smith." I paused and turned away from him. "We only spoke for a second before you abruptly got up and left before slipping your number into my hand. What was I supposed to say "Oh, I can't take this, I'm in high school." I said the last statement a tad sarcastically but it didn't seem to faze him.

Wasn't long before a small grin stretched on his face and he stood, grabbing my hand and making me stand as well.

"Your sarcasm is cute, but you don't have to use it so often." He was smiling.

"This is a pretty open place to meet your student."

"Which is true." Nodding his head but not dropping my hand or creating a space between us.

"Okay. Sooo still haven't told me the purpose of me being here." I laughed lightly. My palm was beginning to become sweaty and my heart was beating so fast. Extremely fast.

"I wanted to see you." He bit out truthfully.

"Well you see me." My voice was barely above a whisper but somehow he heard me and stepped closer.

"This is also true."

Oh God, he was leaning down. Was he going to kiss me? Who am I kidding; he was going to kiss me. He was moving so damn slow. Slower than Carter and this was becoming blissful torture.

Halfway there. I closed the space between our lips and I kissed him before he could kiss me. He was moving too damn slow. Messing with me and I didn't have time for it.

When our lips touched I felt like I had broken every single law in the world and it felt good. His soft lips moved against mine and he wrapped his hand around my waist, drawing me close. So close I could smell him. It was sort of like a corny ass fairytale but it felt so nice.

Here I was in, in a park. Making out with my Art Teacher.

Chapter 9

My dad was back and forth between trips, over and over again. Carter and I had, well I wouldn't say gotten close but we certainly spent more time together. We had made Monday's our movie day. Sometimes Liz would join, other days she was busy. Movie day was always held at my house, seeing as though I think I had the biggest tv.

I checked my hair for the third time in the mirror. My blonde and pink hair was crinkled, just the way Isaiah said he liked it. Although my hair was a little overdone for my simple outfit. My faded blue jeans were splatter with paint and so was my off the shoulder sweater.

I turned to face my new art work on my bedroom wall. The girls hair flowed over her neck line. Colors spilling from every corner, a detail Isaiah had talked me into. Her plump lips were full and shaded in a hint of blue. She had no eyes and most of her was shaded black, making her hair stand out even more. Blue, purple, green, orange, splashes of red and pink. She was beautiful I thought as I placed my hands on my hips proudly.

"Your bed won't be able to be pushed against that wall for at least a day or two sweetheart." Isaiah softly breathed against my neck while wrapping his arm around my waist and pulling me closer to him.

A smiled tugged at my lips and I tilted my head a little to look into his eyes, watching him stare at the art work he helped me with.

We had been spending lots of time together since the park thing. Not much at school, but since my home was usually always free he had been here often. Come to think of it, I had yet to see his apartment.

"Nooooo, I didn't know that Mr. Smith." I smirked and my tone was sarcastic.

"Well I was just saying." He rubbed the back of his neck, which I was learning he always did when he had something to say."

I shifted and turned to face him, snaking my arms around his neck and looking up into his eyes. "What's on your mind."

Surprise took over his face but his expression soon settled before he let out a sigh, "Where are your parents?"

It was cute how nervous he seemed about the question but I was fine with him asking, I knew it would come up soon anyway. "My mom got re-married and usually spends most of her time with her husband. My dad works and is always on trips. I'm old enough to take care of myself so he leaves me here." I shrugged.

His reply was leaning down and kissing me on my lips softly. I didn't allow him to deepen the kiss, so I stepped away playfully. He groaned, but let me slip away before smiling.

"Hungry?" I knew I wouldn't cook, but we could always go out and get something.

He began to fix his jeans playfully and smooth out his tight white shirt with paint all over it. Then running his hands through his short hair before adjusting his glasses. Which were oddly sexy on him today. "Sure, let's go out, paint covered and all." He said sarcastically.

I rolled my eyes. I had totally forgotten about that. But see I could change, he couldn't.

"I can shower really fast and then we can run to your house so you can change no problem." I hoped he would agree. I really wanted to see his apartment. I don't know why but seeing someone's house was just like getting to know them better, to me at least.

A unsure look took over his face and he shifted stiffly before running his hands through his hair one more time. "I can always just call takeout and go pick it up." He suggested.

I huffed, wanting to stomp away and dive onto my bed until he gave me what I wanted. Although that would seem kind of childish, so I refrained from doing so. But damn I wanted to. Instead I just rolled my eyes and crossed my hands over my chest. Attempting to make my face as child-like as possible.

Regardless of my subliminal begging, Isaiah just stared at me. His face unemotional but his lips did twitch into a small smile.

"Fine. But don't take long" He bit out after a few seconds of staring.

I bounced up and ran over to kiss him softly before I sprinted off to my closet to grab a fresh set of clothes. When I skipped back out for my closet I heard his breathless laugh when I slammed the bathroom door.

I emerged from the bathroom, fresh and now covered in a pair of dark wash jeans with a white tank that had holes, placed carefully in a shape of a skull. I paired it with a black cover up and decided to throw on bright red heels.

Fluffing out my hair which still had crinkles. Reapplied my eyeliner. A little mascara and I was ready to go.

Isaiah gave me a nod of approval and we got into his car. Heading towards his apartment across town. The ride was mostly silent, a comfortable silence though. Every once in a while I would sing a song that came on the radio and Isaiah would give me this smile before he would erupt into laughter. Then making joke about my dreadful singing.

When he sang songs, I never made jokes about his singing voice which was way worse than mine I thought silently. We pulled up into a small apartment complex. The fairly large, red brick building looked old but kind of vintage. Perfectly trimmed bushes created pathways which lead to the double glass doors.

Isaiah hopped out of the car and quickly walked over to my side to open my door for me. I slipped my hand into his as we walked to the double doors. Once inside, we stepped into the lobby. I must say, it was completely different than what I expected when considering the outside of the building.

The walls were a pearly white, almost perfect. The ceiling had art work such as random paintings all over it. Small colorful mailboxes lined up in the right corner. A couple sofa's sitting peacefully in the left corner. In the middle there were stairs. Placed safely, was an elevator to get to the higher floors.

"Let's go." Isaiah laced his fingers with mine and led me towards the elevator.

I didn't speak I just followed him. On the way up, an older lady with brown hair and small sprinkles of grey stepped into the elevator. Isaiah addressed her as Ms. Lucy. I'm guessing that's what everyone called her. Her and Isaiah held tiny conversation up until she got off on her floor, flashing me a grin and telling me it was a pleasure to meet me.

I smiled in reply and nodded sweetly. When she stepped off, Isaiah began to roar with laughter. I gave him a puzzled look but still he just laughed. Once he calmed down, whipping some tears away from his eyes and standing up straight he smiled really hard with a face that threatened to laugh again.

"You looked horrified when she stepped into the elevator." He started laughing again.

I crossed my arms over my chest and turned forward to face the elevator doors. He came up behind me and wrapped his arms around my lower waist, pulling me close. His woody scent filled my nose and I couldn't help the smile the spread over my face.

"It's okay. No one knows you here." He reassured me while kissing my temple softly.

I smiled up at him but I didn't speak. I didn't realize how worried I was until every time Isaiah and me went out in public. Even if it was out slightly out of town, I still found myself looking around. Watching to see if anyone I knew would pop up.

The doors opened with a ding and Isaiah grabbed my hand once again and led me to his apartment at the very end of the hall. Apartment 809. Obviously on the eighth floor.

For some odd reason, his apartment door was the only one that was a dark blue. Everyone else's on the floor was a forest green. He let go of my hand and fumbled in his pocket for his keys I guessed. After letting us in, he placed his keys in a bowl that was placed perfectly on a wood table by the door.

Isaiah stepped down from the step by his door and began to walk around the house leaving me at the door. His apartment was built in a sort of open way. The living room took up half of the open area. A medium size dining table with chairs to match was in a corner by the kitchen.

The walls had modest art work taking up most of the space. Isaiah had disappeared around a wall I couldn't see past from where I was still standing. I'm guessing it was his bedroom but I couldn't be too sure.

For some reason I couldn't find it in myself to move.

"Hey, babe. It might be a while I can't find the shirt I want to wear." He shouted from a distance. "Just have a seat or something. Its stuff to drink in the kitchen."

"Oh okay." I shouted back, my voice coming off shaky.

I don't know if Isaiah heard the uncomfortable feeling in my voice but he soon appeared from around the corner. Me still standing in the spot I was when we first arrived. He was shirtless. Oh God, he was shirtless.

I tried not to stare at his chest, but I was staring. His perfectly shaped, tan chest. Regardless of the crappy weather in Michigan, how did he still manage to be tan?

A deep chuckle rumbled from his throat as I looked at up his face. My cheeks turning rosy, trying not to meet his eyes directly.

He stalked up to me and grabbed both of my hands gently. "Are you okay? You look kind of pale." He asked.

I coughed before speaking, trying once again not to stare at his chest. "I'm fine... Go get ready. I'm hungry."

"You sure you're okay?"

I put on the best smile I could. I was beginning to second guess everything I had going on with Isaiah. I mean, after all...he is my teacher.

"Yes, I'm fine. Go." I pushed him playfully.

He kissed me softly and pulled me into the living room before running off to the bathroom to shower. Once I heard the shower running, I took a seat on the leather couches and rubbed my hands on my jeans awkwardly.

After a while, I heard him singing softly. I couldn't help but smile and remind myself to tease him about that later. There were magazines and books placed neatly on the center table of the living room. Remotes to the tv lined up perfectly on the ledge of the fireplace.

I picked up a few books. A fairly large book, with a black cover. Which turned out to be his drawing book. I flipped through the pages slowly. Looking over every single detail in each drawing. My eyes wide and I was amazed. He was way too good to be working at my high school.

He bent over and kissed my cheek. I didn't even hear the shower stop. Let alone hear him getting dressed.

"Having fun?" His voice was joyful but a hint of something I couldn't understand.

I put the book down quickly and shifted towards him. "You ready?" I smiled.

"Uh yeah, sure."

I gathered up purse and stood to my feet. "Where to?"

"Well we could go to Chuck-E-Cheese, you know...for you." He smiled and opened his arms up for me to slip into when I reached him.

I gave a sarcastic "ha ha" but I had to admit it was funny. "Let's go."

We ended up going to a small place right outside of town. Afterwards we went back to my house so we could check on the painting and if it was dry we would move my bed back to how it was.

We sat and talked about ourselves for hours. Shared stuff we didn't know about each other.

Stuff like, favorites colors, food, holidays, candy, movies, etc. He told me about some of his childhood and about art school.

I told him about the days when my parents were married. Outings we used to do as a family. About family reunions. That kind of stuff.

Now we were at the front of the house. Kissing goodbye, and promising to see each other tomorrow after school.

I kissed him goodbye one last time and watched him back out of the driveway.

I closed and locked the door once he was out of sight. Heading to the kitchen to grab a drink. On my way up the stairs, the front door opened and revealed the one and only guy I call my "father."

"Hey sweetheart." He said as he sat his suitcase down and peeled off his coat.

"Welcome home Dad." I said dryly, turning to run upstairs to my room.

"Hey, who was that guy?" He shouted out curiously from the bottom of the stairs.

I stopped in my tracks and turned to face him. "Oh, just a friend. Night."

My heart was beating ten times the normal speed as I ran up the stairs and locked myself in my room.

My dad was careless but I'm sure he wouldn't be okay with me dating my teacher. Isaiah and I had to be more careful.

Chapter 10

"Will you come on?" Carter shouted from my bedroom.

I peeked my head out from the attached bathroom, "Calm your balls, I'm almost done."

"If we're late, it's all your fault. You know you stay a million and one miles away from school, you should have woken up earlier." Carter complained.

I honestly hadn't even been in the bathroom that long. It's just my hair was simply a mess from being crinkled the night before. I didn't have time to straighten it, so today it was going up into a really messy bun.

I turned my nose up at the nest on my head that I was currently calling a messy bun. I applied a small amount of grey eyeliner, maybe to take away from my hair because it was a damn mess. I'm rambling.

Glancing over my appearance one last time. I stepped out of the bathroom to greet a now invisible Carter. Running over to grab my bag, and my art bag.

"You could of at least said you were leaving my room." I said after finding Carter in the kitchen. Figures. "Move over." I pushed him out my way so I could grab some orange juice.

"You two look comfortable." A voice coughed from behind both of us.

Carter and I turned our head to be greeted by my father giving us both stern looks. Carter straightened up his posture and turned to face my father. Me on the other hand, I kept doing what I was doing. Which was trying to get to the back of this large ass refrigerator for an orange juice.

"Hi sir, I'm Carter." He walked over towards my father and extended his hand.

My father over looked Carter before letting his hand shake Carter's firmly. "Just call me Stacie's dad. Sir is too formal."

Carter nodded in response. "Let's go. Bye dad." I moved around Carter and my dad and attempted to head for the door.

"Hey, you dont look like the guy that was leaving the other night!" My dad shouted when me and Carter neared the door.

My heart dropped in my chest and my eyes widened to look at my dad. "DAD!"

Carter gaze flickered between the two of us and he smiled at me before turning fully towards my dad. "No, Uh...Stacie's dad. I'm not the guy who was leaving your house the other night." The amusment was clear in Carter's voice and written all over his face.

My dad had basically just ruined everything. I grabbed Carter by his arms and pulled him out the door and into his car.

"Get in, let's go." I ordered and invited myself into his car and waited for him to get in.

He laughed and climbed into the drivers side, starting the car and pulling out of my neighborhood before even saying anything.

"So when were you going to tell me?" His voice was still amused but his hands tightened on the steering wheel so hard until his knuckles turned white.

I could go about this two ways. I could tell him I was dating my art teacher or I could pretend I had no idea what he was talking about. The second choice worked. I could stretch this on until we got to school since we weren't far away and we don't have any classes together.

"Oh My God, is that Paramore of the radio!" I reached out to turn up the radio but he quickly slapped my hand away, and turning the radio off completely.

"Seriously."

"I don't know what you're talking about." I crossed my arms over my chest and stared out the window.

"Stacie, be serious. Your dad wouldn't make that up." And the amusement was back.

"It was just some new guy from up the street asking if I seen his dog. It was late out and kind of cold so I welcomed him in for tea. Happy? Dad just thought it was something going on." I lied quickly. Good one. Good one.

He just busted into laughter. "You're so lying. But I won't push the issue."

After Carter's small fit of laughter we pulled up at school and went our separate ways. I met up with Liz after first block and we went to Art class together.

"What has your sexy ass been up to?" Liz hit my shoulder with her's after we sat down at our station.

I shot her a crazy look and thought back to how my hair was today. "What's wrong?" I asked.

She bit her lip nervously, "What are you talking about?"

"As we all know, the art contest is coming up soon." Isaiah said loudly to get the classes attention.

The class didn't exactly respond so he went on anyway.

"I was hoping to have some of my students enter." Crickets. "Creative expression is always asked for and no one is going to tell you that your view on something artistically is wrong." Still no one said anything.

"Okay, Stac. I mean Stacie." Isaiah's face turned a bright red and his greyish, hazel eyes widened with shock.

I felt my cheeks flush and I looked around the classroom nervously. "It's okay to call me Stac, everyone else does." I lied, no one really called me Stac but close friends, not even my Dad.

But hey, he was kind of my boyfriend. People at school couldn't know that though.

He flashed a nervous smile but continued anyway. "Like I was saying, Stacie, do you want to be in the art show this year?"

I looked over at Liz who seemed to be in her own world and picking with her nails. Kind of like the rest of the class.

"Only if Liz does it with me." I beamed and looked over at my friend who was kindly giving me a death glare.

"Okay, Lizzy, what do you say? You and Stacie in the art show this year?"

Before Liz could answer, I answered for us. "We'd love to." I smiled really hard and Liz let out a growl of disapproval.

"Great." He clapped his hands together and began to move behind his desk. He walked over to our station and handed us the forms for the show.

"Don't worry, Lizzy. You'll do fine." He said when he gave her the form after slipping me mine with a small note tucked secretly under it.

Meet me after school today. Wait, and then meet me here.

At some point in the class I nodded his way and let him know I got the message. The rest of the class went slowly and we didn't do much.

"I hate you so much, Stac." Lizzy expressed once the school day was over.

I smiled at her, but she owed me one. "You've been keeping secrets, so its only fair that you do this art show with me to make up for it." I knew I was being kind of hypocritical because I hadn't told her about Isaiah and I, but that was different.

"I have not. But whatever. I'll just enter something you've drawn into the art show because you know I can't draw and I can't paint anything but my nails."

I giggled awkwardly and stared at my phone for the time.

"Stac...." Liz said in an annoyed tone

I looked up at her and shut my locker before she could get out any words. "If you see Carter, tell him to wait for me. I have something to do." I kissed her on the cheek and stormed off, not in the direction of the art room. She'd know I was going to go see Isaiah.

After the halls cleared a little and most of the teachers were either locked up in their rooms or gone, I made my way back to the art room.

The dull halls seemed much bigger without being filled with untamed students. Isaiah's classroom door was slightly cracked so I just assumed it was okay for me to enter. Wrong.

I had stepped into a meeting with another teacher. Who knows what they were conversing about but the conversation came to a hault when I entered and closed the door.

Both of their eyes shot to me and Isaiah fought to keep his cool. I had seen the red headed teacher before but I'd never had her class. I'm not even sure what she taught.

Think fast. Think fast. Dammit, today wasn't my day.

"Ermm, hi. I was just coming to talk to Is...I mean, Mr.Smith about the Art Show but I can always talk to him during free period tomorrow." I inched towards the door again, hoping my face didn't have LIE written all over it.

"Oh, its fine. I was just leaving." Her voice was soft and sweet, didn't match her firey red hair at all.

"No, it's fine. Continue. I'll talk to him tomorrow." I slide out of the room and waved bye to the both of them before letting out a breath I had been holding since I stepped foot in there.

Carter was still in the parking lot, well at least his car was. His car was fairly clean for it to be winter time, but hey it was just like Carter to take time to clean his car but not comb his morning hair. I walked up to the car but Carter wasn't anywhere in sight.

I called him a few times, but no answer. Snuggling up in my coat, I was really beginning to get cold so I called again. He picked up but hung up quickly after saying he was on his way before I could get a word out.

Carter black pants came into sight first as he came around the corner of the school. Curse him and his slow ass, walk my hands felt like freshly frozen popsicles now.

"Speed up!!" I shouted but my voice didn't come out as strong as I wanted. Maybe, just maybe my vocal cords or something were frozen by now. Okay, too far.

"Sorry for the wait, I had to do something." He said unlocking the car and getting in as I did the same.

"Like what?" I asked

"Nosey, you didn't tell me what took you so long." He shot at me, starting the car and driving off.

"You didn't ask." I pointed out after turning on the heat and placing my hands over the vents.

"Cause I didn't wanna know." He stopped at the red light.

That made no sense but I wasn't going to push myself into having to explain why I was late getting to the car today.

"My house or yours?" He asked, changing the subject thankfully.

"I bet my dad is still home, so yours. I've never been there before."

"Okay, cool." He did a U turn in the middle of the street and hit the gas heading in the other direction.

"Showing off?" I smirked.

"Just a little." He glanced at me with a smile glint in his eyes.

We laughed and made jokes about students at the school for the rest of the ride to his house. We turned onto a street with middle class homes and I was curious to know which one was Carter's. We had been friends for a few weeks now and I didn't know much about Carter. Come to think of it, I dont even know what his last name is, let alone his middle name.

"What's your middle name?" I blurted out.

"Don't have one." He said in a serious tone.

I turned my head his way and glared at him with disbelief. "You're lying!"

"Nope." He said popping the P. "I'm really serious. Parents didn't give me one."

I let it go although I was still in shock. Everyone has a middle name. Well, I thought everyone did. We had been driving this street for a while and I didn't realize it was this long.

"Carter, where are we?" I asked quietly.

"Close to my house." He said calmly.

"But I've seen that blue house about three times now, which one is yours?"

His face went pale and he took a deep breath. "It's the tan one with white trims."

I searched for the house he was talking about and realized we had been driving up and down the same street this whole time, it wasn't long he just didn't want to go inside.

"Okay, then park and stop wasting gas." My tone was questioning and he pulled over and looked at me.

Turning the car off, he shifted towards me a little to get a better view. His face was expressionless but he looked pale. "See the purple car?" I nodded in response. "That's not my dad's car. And I can't fully remember but it looks like my mom's."

I gave him a puzzled look and that made his expression go from blank to annoyed. "She left my freshmen year. I don't know if it's her for sure, but I'm like eighty percent sure that's her car. And if I'm right, I don't want to see her."

I wanted to meet her but I didn't say anything because I could tell by his pleading voice he wanted to be anywhere but here right now so I dropped it. Plus this had to be my first time hearing about this for a reason, so I wouldn't push the issue.

"Sleepover at my house?" I smiled and leaned over, starting the car again.

Chapter 11

The rest of the week went by pretty fast...I'm lying. It was now Friday and it felt like it took years to get here. I sat in my last hour staring at the clock because I had nothing better to do. I was beyond over the work and my teacher was going on and on about something that happened during his wife's pregnancy. Excuse my French, but he knew no one really gave a damn.

Brushing my bangs out of my face for the hundredth time today, I took a deep breath. I tried scribbling in my notebook, fail. I tried listening to music, even though it was against "class rules". Hell, I even tried reading a book. Don't ask where I got the book from, I have no idea. But class was still going by slow.

If you looked around, everyone was doing the same thing I was doing. Sitting. A hand and a deep voice appeared right in front of me. I must of been day dreaming cause I hadn't even noticed.

I looked up to a settle smile and greyish eyes. I tried to hold in my smile because other students were around, oh yeah, so was my English teacher. I hadn't seen Isaiah in a few days and we had made it a rule not to text too much.

"Hi. Stacie, I was wondering if I could see you in my class-room. We need to discuss the art show." Isaiah said.

I gathered my things slowly but lord knows I just wanted to get the hell out of this boring ass English class. Mr. Green let me go with Isaiah willingly. The man didn't like me too much anyway so I'm pretty sure he was happy to see me go. Along with the rest of the class cause once again, Lizy was nowhere to be found.

Once we got to his classroom he closed the door just slightly, leaving it open, but not enough to see inside. I sat down quickly on the other side of his desk and waited for him to join me.

The weather seems to lighten up a little, but knowing Michigan it was still cold outside. Isaiah came over and sat across from me and just stared. Which was beginning to become uncomfortable.

"So what can I help you with Mr. Smith?" I asked in my sweet, sarcastic voice earning me a slight smirk from him.

He looked around kind of nervously before speaking to me in a low tone. "Well, I just haven't seen you in a while. Last time I seen you couldn't get out of my sight fast enough."

I shrugged nonchalantly, "You seemed busy." Fiddling with small objects on his desk and attempting to avoid eye con-tact.

His left brow lifted but he didn't say much more other than, "I wasn't."

"Wanna do something today, later?" I asked

"If Im not busy, sure." My eyes shot up to his to see if he was serious cause his voice didn't sound too playful.

"Busy doing what?" This was becoming repetitive and it was starting to annoy me.

"Adult stuff." He laughed while I rolled my eyes.

I just looked down at my phone for the time, slowly grabbing my bag before leaning over to plant a kiss on his cheek. "Class is almost over, I better go."

I turned to walk away but he grabbed my hand before I could get too far. Standing within seconds, he pulled me to him gently and kissed my lips. It was fast but soft. Nice, but I was still annoyed. The bell rang.

I kissed him back quickly while stepping out of his hold because the last thing we needed was a student to see us. Let alone a teacher.

When I got to the door he playfully shouted, "Art Show is next week."

I chuckled mildly and threw up my hand as an okay. Here I was chuckling and not paying attention to anything around me. I barely made it out the door before I bumped into what I assumed was a tall man. Well, he was taller than me because my face was planted in his chest in a matter of seconds.

I really hope it was a man because I didn't feel any boobs and if this person did have boobs, they weren't very inviting, I thought to myself. Stepping back, I fixed my shirt before looking into the person's eyes.

His hair was long and messy. It looked unwashed, greasy. I grimaced inside my head but I tried as hard as possible to keep my face expressionless. His eyes were a deep blue and his mouth was just there. Straight almost. His face was expressionless like mine but calm. He had on all black and a leather black jacket.

"Excuse me." I spoke quickly because he didn't exactly look like a student.

"Excused." His voice was deep but he didn't even really look at me. "Now, excuse me, I need to talk to him." He looked down at me and smirked.

I scooted out of his way. I had a bad feeling but I ignored it and went about my day. I went to my locker to grab my things, I was over this school day. Seeing no point to be there, I slipped on my coat and headed for the front entrance.

I was kinda over high school.

Chapter 12

I was rolling around in my bed, lost in my forest of fluffy white pillows, smiling at my pleasant dream when a big monster decided to ruin it all. The doorbell. It quickly woke me up but I kept my eyes closed. I was laying there hoping this disturbance would just assume no one was home and go away.

Once again it was just me in the house so I knew there was no chance my dad would magically appear and get the door. Finally opening my eyes, my eyes went directly to the clock. It read eight thirty, AM of course. Considering the time, that only made this disturbance much worse. Resulting in me being more annoyed than before.

The doo bell went off again then again, oh and again. I pushed my blanket off of me before hopping out of bed in a hurry. Whoever this was really was about to regret waking me up this early on a weekend.

Drawing pencils and a few tubes of paint covered my bedroom floor. I had been working on my project for the

Art Show all night before crawling into bed at four in the morning. This meant I'd only received a few hours of sleep. Probably why I was now so cranky and upset about this disturbance, my sleep was just getting good.

I'm pretty sure my hair was a mess and my tank top way twisted. I still had on my painting clothes from yesterday. Sleep heavy on my face; I stomped down the stairs as the doorbell went off over and over again.

I swung the door open and one could only imagine my facial expression. I was beyond pissed. Especially since I know whatever he had to stay could've waited until noon.

"Carter, what do you want this early?" I growled and blocked the doorway, intentionally leaving him outside.

His brown hair was messy but that was usual for Carter. He was fully dressed and his body wash hit me with full force. Who the hell gets up this early on a Saturday? Better yet, who looks this cheerful, this early, ON A SATURDAY!

With a big smirk on his face, he took in my appearance, "Someone isn't a morning person."

"We both know that already, Carter. What do you want?" I bit out as calmly as I could.

"Get up, get dressed. We're throwing a party tonight. Your place. No, I'm not asking, I'm telling." He pushed me out the way as he spoke, welcoming himself into my home. Completely ignoring the fact I was clearly still tired.

"Only thing I'm doing today is sleeping. Get out Carter; come back when I call you. IF I call you." I whispered the last part as he walked around my living room, face full with ideas.

"Live a little, Stacie. We need a break." He said cheerfully while still walking around my living room.

Carter wasn't going to leave until I agreed to this part idea of his.

"No one from school even knows where I stay." I pointed out.

"Sure they do. I told them all yesterday." He shrugged his shoulders before glancing at me and walking into the kitchen.

"You didn't! You didn't even ask me first. Then you dance in here at eight in the morning and expect me to be okay with a party that you seem to have already planned. With or without my approval." I began to rant and it didn't seem to faze him at all.

"I DID! You need a break. Everyone at school needs a break. Loosen up Stacie."

"No one at that school even likes me nor talks to me."

"True, but they'll come. Look at where you stay. They're coming." Carter smiled at me.

I rolled my eyes and just walked away. I was fully awake now and figured I might as well get dressed because Carter wasn't leaving anytime soon obviously.

I showered and straightened my hair. I figured I'd clean my room later because apparently Carter and I had stuff to do, as he said.

We went to the store to get a few party things. Meanwhile I asked my male neighbors to move all the stuff out my living room and into the empty room not far from the living room.

I sat in the big part of the shopping cart while Carter pushed me around our local Walmart. We joked and knocked down a few things and I'm pretty sure we had to be getting out of here soon before management found out who was messing up every aisle in their store.

Carter drove so I sat in the passenger seat quietly. We pulled up to a small corner store which I suppose Carter had friends at and they would give us drinks for the party later on today. A few younger guys, maybe twenty or in their early twenties came to the car with Carter and helped him pack all the drinks in the trunk.

They both looked like Carter in a way, but just older. A few of the same features but the two guys had green eyes and brown hair. My guess they were twins but I wasn't exactly sure.

He hopped in the Carter after bidding the two guys good-bye. He tapped his hands on the wheel as we made our way back to my house to set up and get ready. It was around five PM when we got everything done. All that was left to do was get ready and wait.

I put on a pair of white ripped jeans and a baby blue crop top. I was debating about which shoes when Carter welcomed himself into my closet to bother me.

"You've been in this closet for a good hour." He huffed.

"You've been in my presence since eight this morning, I'm not complaining." I turned and shot him a sarcastic smile.

"Some guy named Isaiah keeps calling you."

I stiffened but I tried to hide it. "Family friend. I'll call him back later." Good lie. Good one Stacie, I gave myself a mental high five.

"If you say so." Carter turned and left me alone once again.

It didn't take long for my house to fill up with teens. The music was loud and it was clear half the people already came drunk and ready to destroy every nice thing in my home.

I didn't have many friends but I danced around with a few people I recognized. I won't lie; I had a few drinks and was starting to feel myself.

Honestly, everyone at the party looked drunk by the time it hit eleven, at least to me.

I moved towards the kitchen in a slow pace with the intent to get another drink but a firm wrist stopped me in my tracks.

"Carterrrr! Hi." I giggled.

He looked me over before laughing lightly under his breath. "Okay, maybe you didn't need a party." He whispered to himself.

"Has your hair always been this fluffy?" I ran my hands through his hair and laughed.

Carter moved my hand away from his head and began to lead me to the stairs. Everything moved so fast and my body felt so free. For once I felt like a normal teenager.

When we got to my room, he sat me down on the bed and turned to leave.

"Carter, stay." My voice was low and I suddenly just wanted to sleep.

He looked at me with confusion but he didn't deny my request. Carter laid on the bed and we just laid there in silence for a while.

"Carter....."

"Yes Stacie.."

"Can you do me a favor?"

"What is it first?" He chuckled a little.

"Kiss me."

Chapter 13

The last thing I remember was telling Carter to kiss me; everything seemed to go deathly slow after that.

He stared at me for long moments before he even thought about fulfilling my crazy request. I don't know why I wanted to kiss Carter. Maybe I just wanted to see what it felt like. Oh, or maybe I wanted to figure out if sparks were real, you know, like the ones from the movies. The girl finds her true love on one drunken night. Yeah, anyway.

His hazel eyes shined with indecision and Carter just stared at me. I wasn't sure if I should laugh so he'd think I was playing but he could at least say something soon.

I turned on my side so I was facing him. We laid on our sides in my bed, just looking. Carter didn't say anything for a long time and neither did I, but still, no kiss. What if I smelled like liquor? Hell, I did. He did and he isn't anywhere near as drunk as I am.

"Why?" He spoke softly.

Dammit, out of all the questions. "Because I want you to." I said just as softly. Hey, it was all I could think of.

In mere seconds Carters lips crashed down on my own. The movement was aggressive but still a tad gentle. His lips felt like velvet, and he tasted like liquor (but I expected that).

His tongue slipped inside my mouth and I don't know if everything seriously got hotter or if it was just me being a girl. What was he thinking? What if someone walked in? Why hadn't I returned Isaiah's calls? Okay, I'm thinking too much.

Carter's body suddenly towered mine and I widened my legs for his slender body to fit, never breaking the kiss. We kissed harder as his hands went up and through my hair. I whimpered and flipped him over, me now being on top.

I wanted to laugh at his surprise but my lips were kind of busy right now, so I just smiled and he did the same. We rolled around a few times more before the impossible happened.

I felt the plush carpet against the visible part of my back. Carter's body crushed mine and we laid there in shock.

"We rolled off the bed..." He said slowly. He was breathing harder than usual and his face looked confused.

I erupted into laughter while Carter just stared at me with a blank face. I laughed loudly while he just looked at me. I don't see how he didn't find this funny. My bed was huge so I couldn't see how this was even possible or how we couldn't have noticed we were close to the edge.

Eventually Carter joined me and laughed just as loud. We laid there, him still on top of me and laughed until each one of us were red and breathless.

"Get. Off. Me. Carter." I spoke slackened because his weight was really starting to get to me. For such a small guy, he was heavy.

I helped him off by pushing him to the side and getting up before he could see my facial expressions. The humor had worn off and I think so had the liquor. I kissed Carter. Carter kissed me. WE KISSED!

I wanted to jump up and down like a middle school student but then he would probably think I'm still drunk and leave. I climbed back on the bed, legs first and laid down on my side again. Brushing my bangs out my face, I felt the bed push down and his presence was close once again.

His arm wrapped around my waist. Warm breathing danced on my neck as he moved my long hair out the way.

He planted a small kiss on my neck and I melted. I had to remember this was Carter. My friend. That's it, my friend. We shouldn't of kissed and if he kissed me a few times on my neck, we shouldn't do what comes from that either.

This had to stop. I didn't want it to. I basically asked for this. I did ask for this. Why did it feel so good? I knew I couldn't do this yet I was willing to do it anyway. I was forgetting all about Isaiah.

He hadn't talked to me since the whole classroom thing, and the weird biker guy. I was still mad about that, which was partly why I didn't answer his phone calls.

I didn't want to be with Carter, I wanted Isaiah but right now it doesn't seem like Isaiah has much time for me.

Another kiss appeared on my neck again and I let out an uncontrolled sigh.

"Should I stop?" He threaded around the question carefully as his hand moved from my waist to a little lower, pushing my jeans down a tad.

"You don't have to, but you can if you want to." I said breathlessly.

This was probably about to be a mistake, but I didn't care anymore.

Chapter 14

"You don't understand!" I shouted into the phone, suddenly losing my cool.

"No sweetheart, you don't get it." My dad's voice was stern and I could just imagine his face red while clenching his hands.

"It wasn't my fau-"

"Then who's was it? You and I are the only two souls who stay in that house, and before you start with the fantasies, ghosts aren't real. We are the only LIVING souls in that house, and it damn sure wasn't my party Stacie." He yelled into his phone.

"But do you seriously have to keep me locked up in the house for a week?" I whined

"Yes honey, I do. You need to know that throwing a party was wrong. Especially without my permission."

"You wouldn't even know if they hadn't broken a few things. I'll replace them all, Dad please. The art show is this week. Please." I was begging now. I honestly didn't even give a crap about the art show; I just couldn't be stuck here for a whole week. That's boring.

"With my money Stacie? You don't have a job so technically it would just be me replacing things I already paid for once." He chuckled.

A chuckle, I could get out of this. "Please, you can let your staff take a week off and I'll just clean up behind myself. That's punishment enough right?" I crossed two fingers, hoping he just agreed and I could hang up the phone now, ending this hour long debate.

"Fine Stac, I'll be home in a few days."

My line beeped again, the screen of my phone lighting up with Isaiah's name. "Okay Dad, I'll see you then. Love ya." I clicked over before he could reply and greeted Isaiah like normal.

"Hey, mind opening the door?" Isaiah spoke softly and slow.

I got up off my bed and peered out the bedroom window to see him inside his car, waiting patiently in my driveway.

"I could if you tell me what I've done to deserve such random visits?" I joked, still looking out my window.

He gave a little laugh and climbed out of his car. "Stop being silly and come downstairs to open the door."

I made a face as if he could see, hanging up the phone to go greet him properly at the door. My hair was a mess and my face was makeup free but I'm sure he wouldn't care much. The house was finally clean and every trace of teenager that once was all over my house is now gone.

After rushing down the stairs, I pulled open the front door, presenting me with an oddly tanned Isaiah for it to still be kind of cold in Michigan.

"Well are you gonna let me in or just stare at me?" He flashed a big smile, dimples appearing and his glasses moving upwards on his face a little bit.

An automatic smile spread across my face so I let him in. I suddenly felt bad for kissing Carter. Before the liquor wore off I was willing to do more but in the end we only made out for a little while then he retired to the guest room down the hall and was gone in the morning when I woke up. With a massive headache if I must add.

All I wanted to do was focus on Isaiah now, talk to Carter and get back to just friends.

"We haven't talked in days and all I get is a smile?" He mocked disappointed and laughed once again.

"What? My smile isn't good enough now?" I played along, giving off a laugh of my own.

"Beautiful it may be, it's not enough." His smile slowly dissolved, his expression quickly turning arousing. "I've missed you and you just keep ignoring me, Stacie." One foot moved in front of the other and he closed the space between us.

I looked up at his slender frame, serious face, and all I felt was guilt. He began to lean down, I knew he was going to kiss me but I just couldn't right now.

I stepped back a little, causing my body to push against a small end table place conveniently by the door. Note the sarcasm on conveniently.

Isaiah stared at me with confusion. I was annoyed with myself for being so indecisive. I didn't have to tell him. He doesn't tell me everything. I doubt he took us seriously anyway. I mean, I am his student. He couldn't possibly be serious about building a relationship with me.

"I kissed Carter." I blurted it out as quickly as I could, avoiding any eye contact with him the second the words slipped out of my mouth.

I wasn't looking but I felt his eyes staring at the top of my head. I didn't know if silence was a good thing but I was beginning to become uncomfortable. What if he got mad? What if he has some kind of crazy temper and he hit me? I mean, no one else was here. He could kill me and get away with it. No one knew about us, not even Lizzy.

It felt like minutes went by before he actually opened his mouth to say something. He stepped back, creating a new awkward space between us. Once space was created, all he did was laugh, loudly.

Blinking a few times, I brought my gaze back up to him in shock. He was laughing. That was funny to him?

Isaiah closed the space between us once again, pulling me into a light hug. "Aw Stac, that's okay." He chuckled once again before drawing me to arm's length so he could see my face.

"Don't look so surprised, I'm truly fine. I'm not mad or anything. You're young. We were fighting, kind of. I get it, it's fine."

I stared at him in disbelief. Easier than I thought.

"Well wanna go up to my room and see my entry?" It was weird he didn't care about my kiss with Carter but I wasn't going to force him to care about it. It was the past now.

I took hold of his hand and gently yanked him towards my room.

"I really shouldn't see it until the show, no other art teacher involved in this art show has seen their students work." He pointed out but was walking along with me anyway.

"I'm pretty sure no other art teacher is involved with their art student nor randomly shows up at their house without warning." I shot back playfully. "Why did you come over anyway?" I asked once we reached my room.

My painting was on the more empty side of my room, away from my bed and anything else so it could dry properly. I dropped Isaiah's hand and he went over to my painting.

He didn't say anything, he just stared for long moments, occasionally glancing my way but still not saying anything. I was nervous. I couldn't tell if his silence was a good thing or if I failed completely and this painting would not get far in this art show.

Biting my nails, rocking back and forth in my spot, feet planted to the floor, I was just about to start twirling my hair when he spoke.

"Stacie." His voice was soft and hushed. Isaiah's hand rubbed his face and I grew more nervous within seconds.

"It's perfect."

I let out a breath I was holding when his words hit the air. "Thank you." A small, coy smile spread across my face as I walked over to join him in front of my painting.

Isaiah's POV

Any new anger I just had slipped away instantaneously. I gawked at the painting of a girl. Her hair a soft pink, wrapped up and held by a stripped heart shaped pin. The eyes big and colorful, complimented by a dinky button nose. Pouting lips and fingers exaggerated in length.

It was beautiful. So much detail to be done in such little time. All that crossed my mind was how amazing Stacie truly was.

I would hurt her, taint an innocent soul because I couldn't ignore my attraction. I moved my gaze to Stacie once again; she'd joined me and finally returned to her normal color. She was scared, wanting of my approval. She just didn't understand how wonderful I thought she really was.

Maybe that's why I wasn't entirely angry about Carter. I couldn't find it in myself to be when I had kept so much from her already.

My phone vibrated for a third time since I'd arrived, I ignored it again. I already knew what and who it was. I took one last glance at the painting, lacing my hand with Stacie's.

"I have to go sweet heart. I'll call you later, okay?" I pulled her into a hug which she returned quickly. "The painting is perfect." I added.

"You've told me." She smiled.

My hand went under her chin, leaning down and placing my lips on hers.

"And tell Carter you have a boyfriend." I tried to sound as playful as I could but I'm sure she knew I was serious so she nodded in reply.

"I'll walk you to the door." She said cheerfully.

"I'll pick you up in the morning." I said when we reached the door, sharing a small peck before saying our last goodbye with promises to talk later.

Chapter 15

I stared around the room, paintings, sketches, sculptures, and other creative stuff. Everything looked so amazing and compared to my one little painting they all looked professional. I was starting to feel bad for not completely taking this Art Show seriously.

I stood in the entrance of this huge Art building where the show was being held. His hand grasped hold of mine, lacing our fingers. I instantly looked up, snatching my hand away a little too quickly.

He looked disappointed, "Sorry, I just forget sometimes." He gave a bashful smile, tucking his hands into his pants pockets.

"Don't apologize, I'm just always paranoid." I tried to give a bright smile because now I felt bad.

He nodded towards a wall, motioning for me to follow him. I went without any words, following closely behind. My painting mounted up on an all-white wall, next to any other painting, sketch, or sculpture done by someone at our school.

Next to my painting was Lizy's, which I had done also as I promised since I dragged her in this anyway. She still was yet to show up although she texted me and said she was nearby. Paul joined us, standing proudly next to his sketch of famous dead people. Typical but still it was great art work.

Loud footsteps came closer and closer and I knew instantly it was Liz in her combat boots as always. I turned around to greet my best friend who had recently fallen off the face of the Earth.

"Well if it isn't the Ghost of Lizy Taylor." I joked while opening my arms for a hug which she returned quickly.

"I can say the same for you Stac! You've just started to return my text again." She mocked being angry but she smiled in the process.

"I know. I know. I'm sorry." I looked her over and giggled. "Now why are you dressed that way?" I asked, muffling my laugh. She had on pink baggy pants with chains hanging from the side pockets, a black tight-fitted shirt that had similar chains on the shoulders, and of course, her black boots.

"Well I wanted to look like an artist Stac." She laughed herself, leaning closely and whispering in my ear, "Sooo, which painting is mine?"

I had almost forgotten, since we hadn't really kept in touch lately she didn't know what "her" painting looked like. I grabbed her hand, dragging her to the painting mounted on the wall next to my own.

It was a painting of a single girl, standing alone. Her back was turned, a lonely strand of hair hanging loosely from her bun. The rest of the painting was just painted to cover up the white base of the canvas. Simple because I didn't want her painting to beat mine, I was allowing her to claim it as her own, even though I painted it, it would still be her win.

"It's great, yours is too by the way." She shot me a mischievous look and we both laughed.

We took our places next to our artwork, meeting new people, the judges, and holding conversation with each other. Isaiah was with us at first but after a while he disappeared.

A few hours seemed to go by slowly and I was beginning to get tired of smiling and repeating my name. Just as I leaned over to complain to Liz, they sent over one judge to speak to our section.

"We are happy to announce a tie between you two young people." He had a British accent, slim legs but fairly skinny. He looked like the guy from Harry Potter, just smaller, I thought to myself.

"What two?" I asked calmly since he didn't state any names.

"Yourself and this young man over here." He pointed to a guy behind him whom I hadn't noticed until he pointed at him.

I smiled, leaning around the judge to shake the boys hand.

He had brown hair that looked untouched with a few pieces falling freely to his forehead. His eyes were a piercing blue and his hands were soft.

"I'm Stacie." I said when I released his hand from my hold.

"Colton." He smiled. "Nice painting." He added.

"Now that that is over, could you two go find your teachers and meet all of the judges at the front." The British guy said in a dull tone.

Seems like everyone was tired of being here, I laughed to myself. I squealed to Liz and went about my way to find Isaiah.

The gallery wasn't huge but bigger than I would like when I had on heels. I turned corners and spoke to a few more people, asking them if they'd seen my teacher. Most just nodded and said they hadn't seen him.

I grew tired of looking so I stopped in the bathroom. The bathrooms had sofas so I took it upon myself to sit down and rest. I slouched down a tad until I heard a voice coming from the biggest stall.

"You have to tell her now or I will."

I sat up.

"It's not fair to me and frankly it's not fair to her either."

I covered my mouth so my breathing couldn't be heard.

"I'm not going through this any longer, seriously. Tell her!" She shouted now, unlocking the bathroom stall.

I got to my feet, hiding behind the wall so I couldn't be seen when she walked out of the stall.

"You're stretching this."

I got bored and left the bathroom, running my hands over my skirt.

"I can't tell Stacie, Lillia-"

His words were cut off when he seen me, hanging up the phone and staring at me.

I stopped in my tracks, glaring up at Isaiah who looked completely caught off guard.

"It's really not what it looks like." He started.

I laughed, why? I have no idea. I didn't know what was going on but I'm pretty sure he was just talking to the same lady that was in the bathroom.

"I was just looking for you to tell you it was a tie; they need us all at the front." I whispered almost, turning on my heel and heading to the front for myself, not saying another word to Isaiah.

Chapter 16

I couldn't believe him. I finally understood why he didn't get all worked up over me kissing Carter; he was seeing other people anyway. Well at least that's what I assumed from the little bit of the conversation I did hear. I didn't want to hear his explanation, so I stormed off.

I was now talking to the judges, discussing with them what to do since we had a tie and it had never happened in this art show before, therefore, it was only one prize. Colton kept trying to give the prize to me even though neither of us really knows what the prize is yet. All I was thinking about was Isaiah. I hadn't seen him since I stormed off although he was supposed to be up here with the judges, Colton, and I, he wasn't.

"Look, just give the prize to her, it's cool. I'll just tell everyone I won first place but gave the prize to the other person who won first place." He flashed the judges and I a grin, shoving his hands in his pockets.

"But I don't think that's fair." I protested. "We both won, so either we both get something or neither of us get anything." I finished, crossing my arms over my chest.

The same British judge that came to inform me that I won took a deep breath and just stared at Colton and me, not saying anything. The other judges, a young female and an older guy went back and forth just like me and Colton were.

The arguing had been going on for a while so everyone else who took part in the Art Show started to slowly leave. Some collecting their art, others left theirs, not caring enough to go through the trouble of moving it and/or taking it down from the wall.

It was then I remember I rode to the Art Show with Isaiah. I cursed under my breath, fanatically looking around for my phone or any sign of Liz.

"Are you okay?" Colton asked, eyebrow rose with a slight smirk plastered on his face.

I blew my fallen bangs out of my face, making eye contact with him. "I'm fine. I just need to find my best friend or at least my phone." I said peeking over his shoulder to examine the rest of the gallery.

"Must be important." He laughed, "You look stressed."

"Unless you're gonna help me find my friend or my phone, shut up." I snapped.

Throwing his hands up in the air but still smirking just a tad. I growled and stormed off. I heard the judges calling after me but I threw my hand up in response, shouting for them to just give him the prize, whatever it was.

My day had quickly turned into the most annoying day of my life. Well maybe not my life but week at least. I yanked my hair out of its bun, shaking it a little so it would fall carelessly around my shoulders.

I cursed under my breath again when I realized Lizy was long gone and so was anyone else I knew. However I found my phone, dead. Great, I thought, shoving my hand through my hair for a least the hundredth time.

"Do you need a ride home?" A voice from behind me spoke quietly.

"I don't know you Colton, so thanks but no thanks." Shaking my head to deny his offer.

"I'm not some crazy sexy serial killer Stacie." He joked.

A sly smile sat upon his face when I lifted my head up to meet his gaze. His smile causing me to also smile, just slightly.

"Never said you were a serial killer," I laughed. "I just said I didn't know you."

"Well if I'm not a serial killer, what other reason do you have for not letting me at least take you home?" His head tipped to the side as he looked at me.

"You could be a rapist." My voice steady although I was only joking.

You could tell by his sudden facial expression he didn't know I wasn't serious. His left foot shifting to position in front of his right, creating an awkward stance.

"Colton, I'm only joking, don't look so guilty." I said laughing.

"Good one." He bit out while smiling a tad. "So do you need a ride or no?" He asked once again.

I glanced over his appearance one last time, getting up from my seated position on the floor and giving him a nod. "I'll let you take me home, but don't try to come in." I winked, walking ahead of him to the front entrance.

When we reached outside the somewhat cold air hit my face, chilling my body almost instantly. Colton began to walk in front of me, leading the way to his car.

We reached a bright blue BMW, clicking a button to unlock the doors as he went over to the driver's side. Myself climbing in cautiously on the passenger side.

"You do drive safely right?" I asked while clipping on my seat belt. He only laughed in reply then sped out the tiny parking lot.

"I'll take that as a no." I whispered, gripping onto the seat a little, directing my gaze out the window for most of the ride. We sat in a comfortable silence after I gave him directions to my home.

The gallery was kind of a long way away from my home so we would be in this car together for at least forty-five minutes.

"So which painting was yours?" I broke the silence between the two of us.

"I don't paint." He chuckled.

"So what did you do?"

"The sculpture that was right by the front entrance was mine. The big one of the little boy with wings."

"You're joking." I said shaking my head, looking at him.

He looked amused by my surprise. "No, I'm really serious." He turned the corner, entering my neighborhood.

"It was really amazing." I said when he pulled into my driveway and turned off his car.

His eyes were set on my front door, grinning somewhat. "So you're the one who just threw that party." He said quietly, not really asking, more like he was talking to himself.

I planted my hand over my face, "Yeah, what do you know about that?"

"My uncle threw a big fit about the loud music. Went on a long rant all night and I had to listen to it." He laughed faintly.

"Mr. Turner?" I questioned.

He nodded his head as an answer. "I just moved in with him for the rest of the school year."

"I've never seen you before."

"Likewise, not like I'm sitting outside." He looked over at me, smiling.

"So, I'll see you at school?" I inquired, leaning more towards the car door.

"Maybe, I haven't exactly picked a school yet."

"How did you enter the art show if you aren't enrolled in a school?" I scratched my head in confusion.

"I was already signed up when I moved here since my mom only stays in the next town over, I was still allowed to be a part of it even though I'm not enrolled in my last school anymore." He explained while I gave him a puzzled look. "Make sense?"

I nodded in reply, unlocking his car door to get out. "It does, thanks for the ride home." I said softly.

"Hey Stacie." He raised his voice a little to get my attention before I closed his door.

"Yeah?" I leaned over, peeking my head back inside the car slightly.

"Who's your boyfriend?"

Suddenly the thought of Isaiah came rushing back and my throat seemed to close up. I stared at Colton for a few seconds, not trusting myself to talk right away.

"I'm single sweetheart." I smiled, closing the door and not looking back.

"It's not that hard Carter, all you have to do is shake it. Stop being slow." I shouted from my bathroom.

"Why didn't you call Lizy to help you with this Stac, you know, because she's a girl?" He shouted back.

"Trust me, I did. She was busy so you were my next choice." I whispered to myself. "Just shake and stop whining" I shouted to him.

Carter was in my bedroom mixing dye. Well at least trying to mix dye but by the sounds of it he was having a hard time.

"Why do you need this much dye anyway? You've already used one bottle, how much more does it take?" He wasn't shouting, but speaking loud enough for me to hear him.

"My tips were pink Carter, it's gonna take more than one bottle to get it back blonde." I laughed, walking into my room to get the new bottle from him.

"Thank you." I kissed his cheek, skipping back into the bathroom to apply the dye.

"I'm going downstairs to get stuff from the kitchen while you do this girl stuff, if you need me, that's where I'll be" He shouted, the door closing shortly after.

Thirty minutes went by. A very boring thirty minutes if I must say so myself. Carter never came back up to my room so I just assumed he was downstairs watching television or something.

I pranced my way downstairs, a towel wrapped snugly around my hair. I went into the kitchen to find Carter sitting at the bar with Liz and they were laughing about something.

"Well what a pleasant surprise." I said while walking over to the bar to grab fruit out of the bowl.

"Well hey to you too." Liz smiled at me snatching away my peach before I could bite it. Biting the peach herself then handing it back.

"I thought you were busy." I said after taking a bite of the peach and sitting down on an empty stool in-between the two of them.

Lizy ripped off my towel and shrugged before saying any words to me. "I finished what I had to do early so I came by. Welcome back Blondie." She laughed, snatching my peach once again.

Chapter 17

A week had gone by since the last time I'd actually seen Isaiah. I know what you're thinking, kind of hard since he's my teacher, false. I just skipped his class the whole week or just avoided going to school at all. If I went I'd just end up in detention anyway because I wasn't exactly in a cheerful, school mood.

It had finally hit me, Isaiah had been lying. About what, I still have no idea. He hasn't tried to reach out to me either. From this point forward I was just considering myself completely single. I didn't need him, I told myself. It was never going to work; I don't know how I was crazy enough to think it would. Isaiah was twenty-five, I was only seventeen, we were just in different places in life. Obviously.

My phone buzzed next to me, ripping me from my thoughts. I'd started to ignore it but whoever it was continued to text me. Deciding to look when the buzzing had finally stopped. I strolled carefully through all the texts I had just received. Most of them were from Liz or Carter, asking me why I hadn't showed up at school yet again. A few from Colton, apologizing for falling asleep last night and not texting me back. None from Isaiah.

Disappointed, I put my phone down. I was hoping maybe just one of those messages had been from him. He could at least say sorry, anything. My phone buzzed a few more times. Instead of getting my hopes up, I prepared myself for it just being my friends.

I opened up the text without looking at the name.

"Stop looking so sad." It read.

I glanced around my room, looking straight at the window to find a smiling Colton. I gave him a slight smile before getting up to open my window. His uncle, Mr. Turner, had given him a room that was directly across from mine. So if I open my window, and he opened his, we could just speak to each other. Even though it was a tiny distant between the two houses, I heard him fine if we both shouted a little.

"Hey." I shouted at him once he opened his window.

"Hello." A grin spread across his face as he looked over the upper half of my body which was visible to him.

"Don't stare at my boobs; it's just a tank top." I joked to cover up my slight discomfort.

"I wasn't staring, I just glanced." He shrugged his shoulders, still smiling.

"Why are you being a stalker and looking at me through my window? Colton, that's creepy." I teased, giving a smile of my own.

"Well Stac, you shouldn't be so pretty." He busted into laughter.

"Very funny." I rolled my eyes.

"Do you want to go down to that cafe' not far from here, my treat." He asked, no longer laughing but still smiling like a five year old.

"Sure, let me change. Meet me outside by my car, if it's your treat the least I can do is drive." I said, and closing my window before he could respond.

I changed into a pair of jeans, a sweatshirt, and a small leather jacket. Although the weather was changing, it was still kind of cold. Slipping on any pair of black shoes, I ran downstairs to meet Colton.

He was already seated on the passenger side when I reached my car, playing with stuff he found somewhere in my backseat.

"I don't know how you always get inside my car. I'm sure I always lock it after I get out." I started the car, glancing over at him.

"You'll never know." He snickered. "Why do you have so much stuff in your Jeep? You're a girl."

"Thanks captain obvious, I know I'm a girl." I spilled out sarcastically. "And it's just art stuff I haven't got out of my car yet, stop playing with it." I added, snatching away one of my drawing books.

We rode the rest of the way in a comfortable silence, aside from the music playing from the radio. I think it was safe to say Colton and I were becoming friends, but I knew he would be going back home once school ended so I won't be getting that close to him.

When we got to the cafe', we seated ourselves. It was full of a bunch of usual people, not necessarily packed but enough people to know our food would take a while.

"So why'd you dye your hair back?" Colton asked while taking a sip of his sweet tea.

"Just got bored I guess and I kind of got tired of people staring at me." I answered, taking a sip of my own drink.

"I personally think you looked better the other way." He kept a straight face.

I didn't respond right away because I couldn't tell if he was serious. I stared at him silently, studying his expression.

He began to laugh and I rolled my eyes, sighing and looking over my menu once again.

"You should have seen your face!" He laughed harder now, turning red even.

"It's not that funny." I growled although I'm sure my face was pretty funny.

The waiter came and took our orders and brought us more drinks. The both of us sat, laughing and making jokes about one another.

I was in the mist of laughing when the bell went off, signaling someone was entering the cafe'. My gaze shot up to the door, halting my laugh, and causing Colton to look over at the door too.

Isaiah began to walk over to our table, whispering little words to himself I suppose.

"I went to your house and you weren't there." He said to me, giving Colton a quick glance, his face paling.

"Obviously." I spat. "What can I help you with?" I asked coolly, sipping my tea.

"Can we talk?" He rubbed his hand on the back of his neck, a nervous look spread across his face.

"I'm listening." I said, still sipping my drink.

"Alone?" He said, looking over at Colton who suddenly looked confused.

"Now you wanna talk." I laughed bitterly. "Well I'm busy, as you can see."

"Come on Stacie, just give me a second." He begged.

I had no idea why I was being this mean when just an hour ago I was sitting around in my room ready to go into a depression. I ran my hand through my hair and bringing my eyes up to meet his.

"I really am busy." I said softly, breaking our gaze. "Try another time." I whispered, not looking up at him again.

"Fine." He turned on his heel, leaving the cafe' the same way he entered.

"So how about we get that food to go?" I looked up at Colton who just looked confused as hell but he didn't say anything.

"Sure that's fine." Colton said, waving over the waiter but never taking his eyes off me.

"I'll be in the car." I said, getting up and walking quickly to my car.

What a wonderful day this was turning out to be.

Chapter 18

Another four weeks had went by and between those four weeks, nothing from Isaiah. He was confusing and misleading and I was over it. I'm lying. I wasn't over it. I sat in my room and I thought about how mean I was to him at the cafe everyday since it happened. He probably thought I was dating Colton and oh my goodness, I'm rambling.

However I did start going back to school and actually going to his class. Not that I stayed in there long, I usually always did something or made up an excuse to leave and Isaiah wasn't hesitant to let me out.

It was like he was over me now. I know we weren't exactly in love but I at least thought he liked me enough to try to fix things. Maybe I was wrong or maybe I just was too mean to him.

"Stacie." I heard my name but I couldn't tell who it was coming from.

I continued making my way up the narrow hallway, ignoring who ever it was that was calling my name. I brushed my blonde bangs out of my face, adjusting my nerd glasses, I heard my name once again.

I spun around, kind of annoyed by my name constantly being called but not knowing by who. The halls were full of teens my age or younger. Loud shouting and all kinds of curse words were being let into the air, everyone's mouth was moving which only made it more difficult to find out who was calling my name.

Giving up and continuing my journey to my locker, someone called my name yet again. I turned around, halting completely. My bangs fell in my face once more, furthering my irritation.

"What?" I shouted causing a few eyes to look my way but everyone else continued on with their conversations.

I glanced around the halls, waiting for whoever it was to reveal themselves. I wasn't going to move until somebody admitted to calling my name several times. The warning bell rung and I planted my feet firmly on the hall floor, waiting until the halls started to become more clear as students rushed to their lockers or classrooms.

The halls cleared somewhat and Colton and Carter came in my few. They were side by side, coming my way. Colton's blue eyes stood out today against his all dark clothes. Carter's expression was unreadable but he didn't look so down today as he had the rest of this week. The two have been spending a lot of time together since they both were around me most of the time. I think they were becoming friends if that's what you wanted to call it.

Colton had only started school here this week and already a few females drooling over him but he didn't really pay it much attention seeing as though majority of the time I was showing him how to get to his classrooms. None of the girls gave me death glares like they do in the over dramatic teen movies.

The boys finally reached me and I was first to speak.

"Don't ever continuously shout my name like that." I hissed, "It's annoying!"

Carter held his hands up as if he surrendered, a smirk appearing on his face before he spoke. "That was all Colton, I told him to stop."

Colton's glare shot over to Carter attempting to look mad but soon a smirk was on his face also. "I'm sorry, you just didn't seem to be paying much attention."

"It's fine." I brushed it off, "Just don't do it again." On a normal day him calling my name so many times wouldn't have bothered me but I just wasn't exactly in a great mood nor did I want to be at school.

"So what do you guys want?" I asked, turning on my heel and began walking towards my locker.

The boys immediately start walking after me, attempting to keep up with my fast pace. Every few steps I glanced over my shoulder, making sure they were still there.

"Well answer the question." I added when I turned my head back the normal direction so I could see my way to my locker.

"Oh yeah." Colton said. "Carter you tell her."

"Tell me what?" I looked back again to see Carter giving Colton a death glare and whispering some words I couldn't hear because of the distance between me and them.

We all turned the corner into another hallway, nearing my locker and the Art room.

The boys grew quiet when we all arrived at my locker. Putting in my combination, it clicked and I swung the door open quickly before turning to look at them. Their faces held secretive expressions and they wouldn't look directly at me.

"Will you two just spit it out?" I growled and rolled my eyes.

"Carter needs to tell you something." Colton started.

I sifted my gaze to Carter, waiting patiently for him to speak. It was my free period so I was in no rush.

Carter bought his arm up slowly and scratched his neck. I hadn't known Carter forever but I know he did that when he was nervous. He did the same thing when he took me to his house for the first time. I knew whatever it was he had to tell me wouldn't be easy for him to say so I decided not to yell at him to spit it out.

Soon enough, Carter began to open his mouth but closed it once more. In the distance I heard a door open and close, my eyes shooting to the sound almost immediately. There wasn't really any classrooms in this hallway aside from Art and with my luck I knew exactly who was now in the hallway.

His eyes connected with my own and I stiffened instantly. Out my peripheral vision, I seen Colton stiffen also. Remembering it was only his first week here, he hasn't seen half the teachers, including Isaiah. He probably remembered him from the cafe' and began to put two and two together.

Shit. This is what I mean by my horrible luck.

Isaiah broke eye contact first, speeding up and walking pass our little group silently.

I couldn't help but feel like I owed it to him to apologize for being so mean . I fixed my nerd glasses and moved my bangs, suddenly feeling self conscious of my appearance.

Both Carter and Colton stared at me now, however Colton stared a little harder than Carter. I gave them both a small, closed mouth smile that I'm sure looked forced.

"Excuse me a second." I said softly, pushing pass the boys. I never took my eyes off Isaiah as I seen him turn the corner. I needed to talk to him, now while no one seemed to be in the hallways.

I walked swiftly away from the boys. "Carter, come over later, you can just tell me then." I shouted back but he didn't reply. He probably didn't have time to because my swift walking turned into a quick sprint.

Isaiah came into my view once again when I turned the corner of the hallway, going the same direction I had just seen him go.

"Mr. Smith!" I shouted.

Isaiah turned around, luckily after one time of me calling his name. He glanced over his shoulder, halting his steps before turning to face me completely.

I stopped running and began walking slow. The man walked pretty fast I thought as I closed the space between us, catching my breath while doing so.

His hair had grew a little and it looks like he hasn't shaved in a few days. Isaiah's eyes looked dull today compared to how I remembered them. I sound like I haven't seen the guy in years, I know.

"How may I help you Stacie?" He said once I got close enough for him to speak without shouting.

"Why are you being so formal?' I questioned before I could bite back my words.

His expression didn't adjust, he just stared at me plainly. When he didn't speak, I spoke for him.

"Well never mind then." I said quietly. "I just wanted to say I was sorry for being so mean to you when you came to speak to me at the cafe', that's all I wanted." I whispered, twisting on my heels to leave.

He didn't speak for a long while. His voice was barely above a whisper but somehow I heard him even with the small distance I had just put between us.

"Who is the guy?"

"Who is the girl?" I asked with my back facing him, I didn't want to see his expression because his voice sounded hurt almost.

"You never let me explain Stac." I heard his footsteps suddenly, him closing the space between us.

Heat from his body transitioned over to mine and his weird cinnamon and vanilla smell filled my nostrils. I mentally smiled, recalling he smelled the same way the first time he kissed me.

"I know all I need to know. I heard it all." I hissed.

His hands laid on my shoulders, forcing me to face him. "No you don't." He said calmly.

"Then tell me the truth." I whispered, affected by his unanticipated closeness.

His large hands cupped my cheek as his thumb found my chin, titling my face up to look into his eyes.

Seeming he had forgotten we were at school or he just didn't care at this moment. If someone caught us, all hell would welcome itself into our worlds. In spite of the risk, I didn't move from his hold.

"It's more complicated than just telling you the truth." He said.

"How?"

"It's more than what you think."

I thought plenty things but only thing that stuck with me was the thought of him having another girlfriend aside from me.

As if reading my mind, he spoke once more. "I haven't cheated on you, ever." He spoke as if we still were together and his eyes shined with truth.

I felt like the dumb teenage girl who was falling for the older guy and believing all his silly lies.

"If you didn't cheat Isaiah, then tell me the truth." I muttered, never breaking eye contact with him.

He moved closer although it didn't seem possible. For this brief second I didn't care that I was at school. I didn't care who seen us. Being near him again made my heart flutter.

"I can't. Not right now."

His oddly cold breath tinkled on my nose and at the moment all I wanted to do was eliminate the tiny space between our lips and kiss him like old times.

Reading my mind, he did exactly that. Isaiah's soft lips meet mine in a gentle but quick kiss and as if perfect timing, we stepped away as the bell rang and students flooded the hallway for their next class.

Chapter 19

"Just come up to my room when you get here. My dad is in his office so he won't notice you and if you do happen to see him, keep your head down and just speak." I told Colton, Carter, and Liz over the phone.

They were just leaving school; I left after the whole hallway thing with Isaiah. I had no need to stay at school anyway, the rest of my classes were over.

They had somehow got in touch with Liz because I had been trying all day. I didn't see her at school but I knew she was either there or out being weird somewhere else.

"We're almost there." They told me, pulling me out of my thoughts.

"Okay." I said then hung up the phone.

I didn't have on any pants so I sprinted to my closet to find some. I slipped into a pair of leggings to match the sweatshirt I currently had on. I ran my hands through my messy hair, pulling up into a high ponytail. Adjusting my nerd classes, I avoided the mirror, knowing I looked horrible but comfortable.

As I was leaving my closet, I heard the laughing three enter my large bedroom. I nodded my head in their direction then plopped down on my comfy bed. The boys were still dressed in the same clothes from earlier and Liz had on all black with her brown hair high in a ponytail like my own.

Carter sat up against the wall and Colton and Liz sat on my bed with me. My gaze focused solely on Colton as he attempted to avoid looking at me. I brushed it off and just assumed he was tired or something.

Once I got comfortable with my back pushed against plush pillows and my legs pulled to my chest, I focused on Carter.

"So tell me whatever you have to tell me sweet cheeks." I laughed. "This better be good."

Liz shifted on the bed, causing me to look at her. She held the same nervous expression Carter had earlier today at school. Everyone being so weird caused my mood to somber up and wait calmly for somebody to say something.

A few minutes went by of pure silence but I didn't force anyone to speak. I refrained from getting annoyed because I didn't know how serious whatever they had to tell me was.

"We don't know how you're going to feel about it." Liz spoke up first.

"Try me." I nodded my head for her to continue on.

"See, it's been a few things we've been keeping from you." Carter spoke. "You've haven't exactly been a good mood lately and we didn't want to just force this on you."

I just wanted them to spill already; I didn't care about the back story. My eyes were shooting around the room to each person who spoke randomly, Colton was completely quite.

"Liz and I.." Carter started but stopped.

"We've been..." Liz continued.

They looked at each other intensely, as though holding a conversation.

"SPIT IT OUT ALREADY!" I yelled.

"We've been seeing each other." They both shouted at the same time.

My mouth dropped slightly and I stared at the two of them. I waited for several minutes for someone to say they were playing but neither of them did.

Suddenly, I laughed. Everyone's expression grew surprised as they listened to my laughter.

"That's it?" I clutched my stomach. "That's all you guys had to tell me? That you were dating?" I laughed harder. "You guys are so dramatic. I thought someone died or that Carter needed a place to stay. Hell, I even considered for a second that you were pregnant, Liz." I continued laughing as they all looked at me like I was crazy.

When my laughter died down, I spoke again. "How long?"

"Just a few weeks." They spoke in unison.

"Colton, you knew?" I ignored the other two and looked directly at him.

"Something like that." He nodded his head.

"So you don't care?" Liz whispered timidly.

"No, I don't care." I smiled. "Why would I?"

"Cause we've kissed Stac." Carter said.

"And I was drunk and angry at Is..." I caught myself. They didn't know about Isaiah, none of them. Liz knew that was Mr.Smith's real name and I'm pretty sure she would put two and two together fast. She's weird, not slow.

"Then it's settled" Colton clapped his hands and began getting up along with Carter and Liz.

"You two can leave and go do whatever you two have been doing." I winked playfully. "Colton, can you stay back for a second?" I asked quietly.

"One." He counted out loud and confusion spread over my face.

He tried to leave out the room right after the other two and I understood why he said one. I smiled slightly, "Colton, come back."

He stuck his head back through the door and smirked at me. "Fine. Be specific next time Stac."

I got up and closed the door once I knew Carter and Liz were gone and Colton was lying comfortably on my bed.

I settled comfortably next to Colton on my bed and ruffled his messy hair a little like you would do to a small child. His laugh was soft but boomed throughout my room since we were the only two souls in here. Colton pushed my hand away gently and rolled over to his back, staring up at my ceiling and not saying a word.

The silence between us wasn't uncomfortable but it was unusual. "Why are you acting so weird?" I spoke up gingerly.

He didn't answer right away and the quietness between us two became eerie as I tried to entertain myself by picking at my dirty nails. I stared at the side of his face and watched his chin tighten while his eyebrows rose in confusion.

I sat up from my laying position and pulled my knees to my chest, never speaking, only waiting for him to reply.

"I thought you were smarter than that Stac." He said after what felt like a few more minutes of silence.

"What are you talking about?" I was still playing with my nails, pretending to not have a clue where he was going with this.

"I won't tell anybody you know?" He said suddenly, also sitting up from his laying position.

"Still don't know what you're talking about, Colton."

"Stacie, look at me." Dropping my hand to my lap, I looked at him. His piercing blue eyes appeared more grey today as he stared at me with an unreadable expression.

"I saw the way you two looked at each other. I remember him." He glared into my eyes as he spoke. "Look at me." His voice was ruff however he still seemed to speak so softly.

"It's not what you thin-" I started but he only held his finger up, shushing me.

"I'm not stupid and neither is everyone else in this town. Be smarter Stacie." He deadpanned.

"Why do you care what I'm doing anyway?" I shot out forcefully. I was being defensive because I knew he was right. Isaiah and I weren't doing well hiding anything.

A look flashed on his face which I couldn't quite decipher but it left just as quickly as it came. "I care because I don't want you to get hurt because you think you're just having fun. Going with a teacher isn't smart, at all. I just don't want you to regr-"

I held my hand up, halting his words. I wouldn't regret anything. Even if all this back fired and we got caught or Isaiah actually did hurt me and lie to me, I wouldn't regret this.

"Thank you, but I'll be fine." I said while pushing back new strands of hair that fell from my ponytail.

"It's no problem, just be safe." Colton said, moving his gaze from me to the door. "I better go I guess."

I nodded in reply as we both got up to go to the door. I grabbed his arm, pulling him in for a hug. His fresh scent filled my nostrils while he adjusted to the shock of my hug but hugging me back nevertheless.

"Our secret." He whispered in my ear, sending a weird sensation down my spine forcing me to pull away slightly.

I only nodded my head and stared into his now illegible eyes. Colton pulled my head to his lips, placing a small kiss on my forehead before letting me go completely and leaving my room without granting me with another simple glance.

I stood in my room, confused and surprised by his sudden affection. Taken aback by his random concern, it made no sense to me. But what I felt from his affection, how my stomach tightened and my heart sped up a little, that made no sense to me either.

Chapter 20

I woke up to the loud sound of my father yelling about someone not being responsible. I mentally groaned and put my head under the blanket instantly. It was Saturday morning, two weeks since I got back together with Isaiah. Two weeks of avoiding Colton also. I mean, of course I seen him, we went to the same school, had the same friends, and were neighbors. I just couldn't really face him after I had that weird ass feeling when he did simple things that friends do. I always made up a lie to get out of spending time with him.

I figured since he knew about Isaiah and me, I could tell him I was with him or I was busy with my dad. The lies were working so far but I wasn't sure how much longer he would believe me. As he so kindly pointed out before, he's not stupid.

I couldn't shake the feeling that he felt something too, hence why he left my house in such haste. I'll never know for sure though because I'm not crazy enough to ask. He could have some silly idea that we can be together and I might start to do something else crazy, like consider it.

Being with Colton would be ten times easier and he's never lied to me before. Along with us being the same age, he's extremely cute and he has this wonderful bright smi- Oh my goodness, I'm actually thinking about being with Colton.

I pulled my face from under the blanket and attempted to adjust my eyes to the sudden sunlight that shined through my windows. I could tell my dad was now on the second floor of the house because his yelling seemed to be closer than before. I thought about just putting my head back under my blanket but I knew whatever he was mad about it would only annoy him that I was still in bed.

With that thought on my brain, I hopped out of bed as quick as I could, tested my track skills and sprinted to my bathroom. Avoiding the mirror, I started running water so I would sound like I've been in this bathroom for a really long time.

I brushed my teeth and washed my face. I dreaded opening the door and entering my room because I had a feeling my father was in there, waiting. However, I needed clothes so I could shower. I know it's my room and my bathroom but in this house and the way my friends are, I'd be coming out the bathroom in my natural outfit and someone would walk in, seeing all my goods.

Taking a deep breath, I opened the bathroom door and sprinted to my closet as fast as I could. I'm guessing I was just in a running mood this morning. I rushed around my closet, grabbing random items and reminding myself over and over again not to forget my underwear.

After showering, I got dressed in the random items I picked and began to lay around my room. To my surprise, my father's yelling had stopped and he wasn't in my room hounding me about being irresponsible.

The house fell silent for a good half hour before my father busted into my room randomly. I was dressed and in the mist of painting so at least I didn't look too lazy.

"Your mom should be here to pick you up soon." He looked me up and down, taking in my outfit. "And change clothes, I don't wanna hear her complain."

My eyes grew wide. I hadn't talked to my mom in a few weeks and even then it was only via text messages. "When did she tell you she was coming to get me?" I never looked up at him, I just kept painting.

"I spoke to her this morning, I'm sure you heard." He ran his hand through his hair roughly. "That woman infuriates me. I don't know how I married her." He whispered under his breath.

"Well call her back and tell her I have plans." I huffed.

I didn't truly have plans I just didn't want to deal with my mom today. All she talks about is her new husband and what he does that my dad didn't do. It grows annoying after a few minutes, I'm a teenager and on top of that, I'm her child. I really don't want to hear all of that kind of stuff.

"I'm not going to do that Stacie. You have to go." He said in a stern voice to which I just rolled my eyes.

"Well, I'll just skip out. You can tell her I'm coming though, that way she'll just be mad at you." I turned my head his way and smiled tightly because I knew that would annoy him.

"Stacie you will go and that's final." He raised his voice a tad and tried staring at me with aggression.

I shifted my body to face him slightly; I took in his silly facial expression and began to laugh lightly. My laugh grew from settle to uncontrollable while I felt my face turn red and tears brim my eyes. He was seriously trying to control what I did with my day. That's hilarious.

Getting myself back together, I stared into my father's eyes. Trying to get a grip on the little laughter I had left in me so I could handle this moment properly.

My dad's face held a blank an expression now and he looked bored.

"Stacie, you're going to go." Were his last words, leaving my room before I could get a chance to debate with him on this issue.

I finished up my painting, where it now sat drying by my window. The window was open wide to let the crisp air in because my room's air didn't seem to be drying the painting that well.

My dad hadn't come back in my room since our little conversation. I seriously didn't want to spend the day with my mom so I sat on the phone with Isaiah, trying to figure out if he was busy.

I stood in my closet, searching for something to wear. He had me on hold for about a whole minute and I was beginning to become irritated.

"Hanging up now!" I said in a sing-song voice.

"Wait, no. Hold on." He sounded like he was running. His breathing was labored and I could hear him fumbling around with his phone.

"Then how about getting on the phone and listen to me then?" I rolled my eyes as if he could see me.

"Stac, one second." He said gently.

I huffed but I stopped complaining. I pulled out a blue and grey oversized sweater and a pair of thick black leggings. From the looks of things I wouldn't be doing anything today so I was going to dress comfortable.

"Okay, I'm back." He said while I was in the middle of pulling my sweater over my head.

I couldn't exactly respond so I just made a weird sound, hoping he understood what I meant. Isaiah had become sweeter than usual. He stayed on the phone with me for hours even though we both had school the next morning, him work of course.

I think he was only doing sweet things to make up for the lies he's told me. Even though I still don't fully know what those lies are yet. He claims he's just protecting me but not telling me the truth isn't exactly protecting anything.

"Stacie." He shouted.

By the tone of his voice he'd been yelling my name for a while now so I'm guessing I zoned out again.

"Yes, I'm still here." I grabbed the phone and put it back up to my ear.

"Good, so what were you saying before I put you on hold?" You could still hear Isaiah's breathing trying to return back to normal.

"I was asking you if it was okay if I stop by today. We, I mean, I don't have anything else to do so I was wondering." My voice came off childlike and I mentally cursed myself for sounding so nervous all of a sudden.

He coughed in the background and that's when I start preparing myself for him to lie about being sick or busy.

"You don't think someone will see you coming to my apartment this often?" He whispered.

"Nobody knows me in your building." Was my only reply as I slipped on my boots anyway.

"That's true but you never know what might happen. This isn't exactly a big town." He argued.

I was growing more irritated by the second and I couldn't refrain from rolling my eyes. "It's a yes or no question, Isaiah. Can I come over or today isn't a good day?"

I heard him take a deep breath but as soon as he was about to speak, a small rock hit the exposed part of my neck, causing me to curse quietly.

Turning to face my window, all I seen was a smiling Colton.

"Yeah, Isaiah, hold on." He didn't reply but I took my phone away from my ear anyway.

Taking big steps towards the window and when I reached hearing distance I didn't give Colton any time to speak.

"What the hell is wrong with you? That was a rock! Where on earth did you even get a rock from!? Your room is on the second floor. You're too old to be playing with ROCKS

Colton." I rambled in a yell-whisper kind of tone while rubbing my neck in the spot where the rock hit me.

His only reaction to my boatload of questions and insults was a smile. A creepy one at that.

I huffed, blowing my bangs out of my face. "C, you must be really bored." I said calmly, staring back at his big, bright...but creepy smile.

"You know me so well." He laughed, leaning out his window a little more. "Wanna hang out today?"

I stiffened at the question and bit back the urge to just say yes. It was sad because something in me really just wanted to say yes and forget all about Isaiah who didn't seem to want much of my company anyway.

"What would we do?" I asked.

He just shrugged and moved a strand of hair away from his eyes. "I don't know, whatever teenagers do on Saturdays, or you can just come over and we can watch movies or something."

I thought it over quickly. Solid plans with a guy I'm slowly becoming attracted to or fluctuant plans with my so called boyfriend. Anything beat a day with my mom.

Holding up my finger, telling him to wait a second, I ran back to my phone that I had thrown on the bed before running to my window.

"Hello?"

"Yes." He spoke. "So do you still want to come over?" He asked suddenly before I could get my words out.

Taken aback by his sudden interest, I looked over at Colton who still stood in his window, waiting patiently.

"Maybe tomorrow." I said to Isaiah and hung up the phone before he could respond.

"This isn't a date or anything!" I shouted loud enough for Colton to hear me.

His expression changed into a playful one as he took in what I just said. "Oh, that sucks then." He gave a small smile and nodded his head slightly.

I smiled back in response, gathering a few things to prepare for his house.

"I'll bring the snacks, you find some movies. Meet me at your front door in ten." I said loudly.

"Cool. It's a date." I looked up just in time to see him wink and close his window.

My heart skipped a beat and I smiled a little on the inside. It's a date.

Chapter 21

I met Colton at his door in exactly ten minutes. He was there waiting for me in whole new attire. He no longer had on jeans and a sweater, his chest was covered in a white V-neck that clung to all the muscles he did have, along with some random college logo sweatpants. However, his hair was still as messy as before.

"Well now I feel overdressed." I said as a greeting, pushing my way pass him and into the house.

I'd known Colton for a while now, but this was my first time ever stepping foot into his uncle's home. Everyone usually just hung out at my house.

The door shut softly behind me as I took in the decoration of the house. It looked exactly how I imagined Mr. Turner's house to be. Everything was set up oddly although the house had just about the same structure of my own home.

The windows had large curtains but were currently open to let the sunlight shine in. As far as I could tell, only being granted a small view of a leather sofa, the living room was what being hidden behind two wooden, big sliding doors.

All the walls were painted a boring off-white and the only things truly in front of me were stairs.

"Room is this way." Colton said dryly while walking in front of me to lead the way.

I followed behind silently and didn't say a word until we entered his room. He instantly leaped onto his bed as I stood by the door awkwardly taking in his boyish room.

"Well, close the door and stop staring Stac." He chuckled a little, pushing a hand roughly through his hair.

I nodded and closed the door, but still I didn't say anything. Everything felt weird between us now. Probably because part of me just wanted to ask him if he felt what I felt that one day, although I knew I would never bring that up.

The sound of patting snapped me out of my thoughts, my eyes glancing over to a smiling Colton as he patted his hand on his bed, motioning for me to come sit.

My heart sped up a little at the thought of sitting next to him...on his bed. The room was fairly large, about the same size as mine. There were several doors, which I just assumed hid the bathroom and his closet. The walls were a dark blue and everything in his room was a mahogany, the dresser, bed, end tables, everything.

I walked slowly over to the bed and set down my bag of snacks. His gaze went to the bag, no longer on me. I physically felt my heart slow down. I don't know why I was freaking out like I'd never been around Colton alone before. Where the sudden tingles came from whenever I thought of his name and his smile, I don't know where that came from either.

"Well sit. Damn Stacie you're acting weird." He spoke up.

I quickly sat down next to him and looked his way. "I'm not acting weird." I laughed silently, brushing stray strands of hair behind my ear.

"Surrrree you aren't." He laughed. "So what snacks did you bring?" He asked, reaching for my bag which I immediately snatched up before he could get a hold of it.

I held the bag up in the air, smiling at his random confused expression. "Guess." Was all I said, standing up on his bed so the bag was further from his reach. Thankfully I didn't have on shoes anymore, I thought.

"There's the Stac I'm used to." He whispered to himself, smiling.

"What do I get if guess correctly?" Colton said with a sly smirk taking over his face and his deep blue eyes shined with excitement.

Returning his smirk, my heart hit a hundred miles per hour for the tenth time today as I thought about what he should get if he guessed right. My mind instantly went to a kiss but my rapid thinking stopped when Isaiah popped up in my head.

I was being unfair to him right now. Sure he had lied to me before but to this day, I still didn't know about what exactly. Of course that was because he still wouldn't tell me for whatever reasons, those he wouldn't tell me either.

Besides, Colton didn't know I was starting to like him a little. Hell, I didn't even realize I was starting to like him until seconds ago, literally. I'm sure he was still under the impression that we're simply friends and I have Isaiah.

I was thinking too much.

"Are you going to keep zoning out like that?" Colton asked his expression curious but his voice still held a hint of play-fulness.

I pushed Isaiah to the back of my mind. "Maybe." I smirked, and began jumping on his bed like a five year old.

I jumped for probably a whole minute until I felt my leg being pulled and everything after that moved completely too fast.

My whole body hit the soft mattress covered in a "teen boy" like blanket. My breath hitched in my chest as I felt the sudden weight of Colton holding me down.

He grabbed both of my wrists and held them over my head in a forceful manner. I currently still had possession of my bag but I was starting to highly doubt I would have it for long.

Due to the way I was pulled down, my body laid flatly onto his bed and my legs were bent in some weird way to try to soften my fall. His body was placed perfectly between my legs and suddenly his face seemed really close to my own.

I peered into his eyes for the first time. His eyes were clouded and distant.

"What do I get?" He huffed loud enough for only me to hear, not like anyone else was in the room anyway.

I wanted to speak up and say something playful back but I just kept staring into his captivating eyes. He didn't speak again, just stared right back into my own eyes.

"Just guess." I muttered quietly.

"Gummy worms." He smiled, breaking our stares and looking up at my bag.

I strained my neck in this compromising position we were in to see what he was looking at. Snacks were pouring out of my bag, more specifically, gummy worms.

I grinned, "You cheated."

"We didn't make any rules." He grinned back, brightly. "So what do I get?"

We never moved, shifted, or even attempted to get up from our position and oddly; this didn't feel awkward at all.

"What do you want?" I whispered, looking into his eyes once again.

He didn't speak; he just closed the space between the two of us. His lips set upon mine as I took a few seconds to register what he was doing.

My breathing became labored as my eye lids slowly shut and I kissed him back. The kiss felt gentle while his soft lips moved on mine in slow movements.

The kiss didn't last long but I could still feel his lips on mine.

Colton moved away in hesitant movements and smiled at me. He grabbed the gummy worms from off his bed and lay next to me.

"Now let's watch this movie." Was all he said as he popped a gummy worm into his mouth.

I just stared for several seconds and tried to take in what just happened. I wasn't really worried about the kiss anymore; I was worried about why I didn't feel bad about it happening.

Chapter 22

"Lizzy, I really don't know how it happened, it just did." I huffed into my phone while running my hand roughly through my hair.

"Well I really don't know what to tell you Stac. I kind of saw it coming." She replied

I rolled my eyes as if she could see. "Like you ever take your head out of Carter's ass long enough to notice what's going on with me." I snapped, instantly feeling bad once the words wiggled from my thoughts and out my mouth.

She gasped but I couldn't tell if she was really affected by my sudden rudeness or if she was joking.

"I'm sorry Liz, I'm just really confused." I said softly.

"It's cool. I get it, really." Liz took a deep breath. "I have to go, talk to you later." Hanging up before I could grant her with a proper farewell.

I tossed my phone on my bed, burying my face into my pillows.

"Why me?!" I shouted to myself.

After the kiss with Colton, he went about things as if it never happened, never bringing it up or even acting weird around me. Although it's only been two days and I've only seen him through my window, I thought.

Is he as affected as I am? Did it mean anything? Why didn't I feel bad? I asked myself the same questions over and over again since I got home from his house the other day.

As for Isaiah, we'd been texting but every time he asked me out or asked for me to come over, I made up some excuse. I didn't necessarily feel bad about the kiss right now but I knew the second I seen him, I would begin to.

Regardless of whatever he is keeping from me, no one deserves to be cheated on. I contemplated on telling him but maybe I shouldn't share secrets until he shares his.

I was falling deeper into my thoughts when my alarm sounded on my dresser. Time was telling me I needed to be getting ready for school but I dreaded school for so many reasons. One, I was fucking tired. Two, I was still deeply in my thoughts and didn't want to get out of bed. And three, I would have to face Isaiah at some point today.

However, I reached over and shut off the alarm anyway. Climbing out of bed and heading to the bathroom for my regular routine and a shower.

Once all the normal stuff was done and I was dressed in a casual shirt and a plain pair of jeans, I ignored my hair and let the slight natural wave do whatever it chose to.

I gathered my things then headed to the kitchen for a quick snack before I stepped out the door to begin my long trip to hell (high school).

To my surprise, my dad was at the stove, humming away when I entered the kitchen. It was always odd to see my dad home, especially on a weekend, scratch that, especially on a Monday.

"Hey sweetheart." Without turning around, he spoke.

"Hey dad." I said dryly, walking over to the counter to grab an apple.

"Well someone is grumpy." He joked, finally turning to look at me, only for a second before focusing his attention back on his eggs,

"Just tired."

"Maybe if you didn't spend all night on the phone, you could've gotten some sleep" He chuckled lightly.

I took a seat and bit into my apple, ignoring his last comment.

Moments went by silently, only the faint sound of me biting into my apple and the eggs being cooked.

"You know if you are having boy troubles, its okay to talk to your Dad." He started.

I huffed and rolled my eyes for probably about the tenth time this morning. "Dad, I'm not having "boy troubles." I dramatically made air quotes when I said the words boy troubles.

"That's not what I heard." He sang childishly.

I got up from my seat, grabbing my things and turning to leave the kitchen while my father sat at the table with his eggs. A peaceful look spread across his face and I mentally smiled because even though I was in a horrible mood, he seemed cheerful and that's a version of my Dad I haven't seen in a long time.

"Bye Dad." I waved and sprinted out of the house before he could say much more than a quick goodbye.

The drive to school seemed to go by faster than I may have liked and I actually made it through my first period without going to detention, a personal best.

It was now the part of my day I was dreading since I stepped foot into this place. Second period, Art. This means, Isaiah, and not only Isaiah, Liz as well. Seeing as though I snapped on her this morning our conversation probably wouldn't be all giggles and laughs.

Taking a deep breath, I pushed forward into class. I didn't really look up or glance around the class to see who was inside; I just tucked my hair behind my ear nervously and took my seat. Liz wasn't here just yet and from the sound of the class, no one really was.

"Surprised to see you here." I heard his voice in the short distance.

"Well it is Monday." I said sarcastically, moving my gaze away from my fiddling hands but I still didn't look directly at him.

"Whoa, grumpy." Colton said smiling slightly.

"This isn't even your class Colton, what do you want?" I asked softly, shoving my hair behind my ear again.

"I wanted to give you your sweater." He set my sweater from the other day on top on my table, smiling while doing so.

It took me only seconds to realize what he was up to. Any other time he would have just kept it in his car and gave it to me at lunch or something. Oh wait, or maybe walked across some grass, knocked on my door and gave it to me.

My horrible mood instantly got worse and I looked Colton dead in the eyes. "What's your deal?" I whispered through clenched teeth.

A full blown grin broke out across his face and he leaned down, placing a kiss on my cheek. Colton didn't speak anymore words to me, only turning on his heels and granting Isaiah with a simple head nod and leaving the classroom while other students finally began to pile in.

Isaiah stared at me, not hiding his confusion or irritation. However, that was the last time he looked at me throughout the entire class period.

Class passed by really slow but the rest of the school day went by fairly quick.

After stopping at my locker, I decided it would be best if I went to speak with Isaiah before his mind wondered any more than it already has but when I arrived at his classroom he was already gone.

That was weird but I chose not to pay it much attention. Mainly because I didn't have much time to give it any thought before Colton appeared in my view.

Not speaking, I rolled my eyes and turned the other direction to walk away. I felt his presence behind me but I didn't care much to turn around and figure out exactly what he wanted.

"You don't have to be pissed." He said

"You most likely pissed him off, great job." I muttered, still not turning to look at him.

The halls were empty and there wasn't a teacher in sight. Things were starting to feel like school was over a long time ago, longer than I thought.

"He didn't pay any attention to me." Colton huffed. "Besides, all I did was giving you your sweater back."

"Think about it Colton!" I shouted, stopping on my heels. "How the hell did you get my sweater? I still go out with him you know?!" I threw my hands up in the air dramatically and took a deep breath to calm myself down.

"Kissing you was a mistake, especially if you're going to act this way." I added once I calmed down completely.

Colton opened his mouth to speak but before he could say any words, a tall figure behind him cleared his throat. He looked familiar but I couldn't quite pinpoint where I had seen him before.

"Sorry to interrupt." He started, stepping around Colton completely. "I need to speak with her." The strange man said to Colton. "Privately."

Colton didn't argue, only dismissing himself without even glancing at me one last time.

I didn't know this man and neither did he, how could he just leave me here all alone I thought.

"The names Isaac." The familiar guy put out his hand for me to shake which I did so hesitantly.

Chapter 23

I took a sip of my fruit-flavored tea, shifting my legs in and out of comfortable positions. My arms were feeling weak and I had the worst headache known to man. My bottom hurt from sitting in these old iron chairs, and yes, I'm very much complaining.

Issac had me follow him to this weird cafe that seemed to be located in a part of town I never knew anything about up until now. I didn't know this guy but I agreed because he said we were going to a public place.

Hardly because this cafe had absolutely no customers aside from the two of us. And instead of Issac starting the conversation soon after we got drinks of our choice, we've been sitting here for over ten minutes and he still hasn't said a word or looked up from his phone.

I coughed in attempt of getting his attention and I was seconds away from just kicking him directly in the shin but decided against it when I realized how scary he actually looked.

"Let me properly introduce myself." He started and I cocked my eyebrow in reply.

"Issac Smith, Isaiah Smith's older brother." He said confidently, flashing me a smile that looked dangerously close to Isaiah's.

My breath caught in my chest as I tried to process what he'd just said and I was just utterly confused. I'm sure I looked like I'd just seen a ghost because his smile grew wider if that was possible.

"I'm lost. Isaiah's never mentioned a brother before." I said slowly, still lost in my own thoughts.

"I'm sure he hasn't. It's a lot he hasn't told you about obviously." Issac said.

"How do you even know about me? I'm just his student." I immediately lied.

Issac's chuckle filled the small cafe and his eyes lit up at my statement. "I remember you, Stacie right?" He nodded his head before I could even answer. "No regular student just leaves a classroom looking as happy as you had the first day I seen you. You really should try to hide your guys' relationship better."

I probably should have been speaking up for myself, denying his accusations but it was like my voice had suddenly disappeared or as old people would say, the cat had my tongue.

Already, I wasn't positive if I liked Issac or not. Quite frankly I thought he was strange so far and on top of that, he still hasn't told me why he wanted to talk in the first place.

"Well, anyway, what do you want with me?" I snapped.

"Feisty are we?" He said slyly. "I'm really not the person you of all people should be getting snappy with."

"And why is that?" I rolled my eyes dramatically.

"Because I'm not protecting my dear brother this time."

"This time?" I questioned, all attitude swiftly diminishing and replaced with curiosity.

He only smiled, taking a sip of his coffee. Issac's gaze went back to his phone and he tortured me by not speaking again for what felt like eternity. In reality it was only ten minutes but we all know how I get.

"My brother seems to have a thing for woman he shouldn't be with." He spoke up. "Or this time, young girls."

"Isaiah isn't that much older than me." I shot back.

"Sure he isn't. Anyway, not here to talk about age."

"Then what are we here for?" My voice was coming off angrier than I intended but he was beginning to get on my nerves with all the suspicion.

"You're an eager one." He chuckled lightly, earning a grunt from me in return.

"Let's get this show on the road, tell me what you want already." I said, running a hand through my messy hair.

His eyes followed my movements as he took a deep breath. People were starting to enter the cafe and that was beginning to create small distractions for Issac.

"Calm dow-" He started

"I can always leave!" I said firmly, leaning over to put a hand on my purse that was placed safely on the floor next to my foot.

"You could. But if you were gonna do that, you would've done that a long time ago." Issac pointed out arrogantly.

I slowly withdrew my hand back from my purse, placing my hands softly on my lap and choosing not to speak anymore.

Issac coughed, his expression turning more serious as the seconds went by. "I'm not going to tell you everything; I'll allow my brother to do that."

I nodded in response and waited for him to continue.

"Next time you see him, ask him why he has started the cycle over again, only this time, he's not the student...but the teacher." He said with a smirk plastered on his face.

Sliding his chair back, Issac stood, only nodding his head as a goodbye and did not speak another word to me.

He left me here in my thoughts and if I must admit, I was really at a loss for words. If I understood him correctly, Isaiah had dated one of his teachers before. It made sense, why he knew how to handle our relationship. When to speak, not to text too much, where to meet. It all made sense to me now.

But why wouldn't he tell me that? I wasn't sure how I should feel but I had this strange feeling in the pit of my stomach it was way more to the story than what his mysterious brother Issac had just told me.

Although I wasn't sure why Issac would want me to know so bad and not allow his brother to tell me on his own terms.

It was all just really strange and thinking about it was doing nothing but giving me a head ache I didn't feel like dealing with.

Chapter 24

My head was spinning and the current space where I was laying didn't exactly feel familiar. The sheets felt soft against my body but they didn't feel like my own. Quite frankly at this moment I was too afraid to open my eyes.

A delicate growl came from beside my face, knocking all fear out of me and instantly causing me to snap my eyes open. But still, I was a tad afraid to look over.

"Good morning." He spoke first.

Colton.

My heart sped up and my mind went into full panic mode. How the hell did I get here? How long had I been here? Well, that was a dumb question, he clearly just said good morning. So did that mean I was here all night?

I hadn't been drinking last night, so why the hell couldn't I remember anything?

"Stac..." Colton started, his voice pulling me out of my thoughts.

"Oh, yeah. Morning." I muttered quietly.

I still couldn't find the balls to look at him but I knew it was him. I knew I was in his room, the same blue walls, blue everything.

I probably look horrible right now and I was suddenly feeling self conscious.

"You look fine." He spoke up.

Did I just say that out loud? My gaze fell upon the small clock that was on a table across his room, nine-thirty AM.

"How long have I been here?" I asked him after a few moments of silence between the two of us.

"Since three AM." Was all he said before shifting away from me and sitting up.

I let out a breath I wasn't aware I was holding and finally found the courage to look up at him. Colton's eyes looked tired and his hair was messier than usual. I couldn't see his bottom half because they were covered by his blanket but his shirt was invisible.

"Don't worry, we didn't do anything." He smiled slightly.

I cocked my eyebrow in response to which his smile grew brighter.

"It's kind of hard to do something with a girl who's crying and fully dressed." He joked.

I moved to sitting position, feeling my jeans rub against my body and I felt a strange relief.

"Crying?" I questioned.

He spared me a confused glance, curtly nodding his head. "Crying, you started throwing rocks at my window sometime last night so I went downstairs to let you in." He explained.

"Go on." I urged.

"After I let you in, you didn't say anything, just hugged me and asked me to be a friend. I'm not sure if you were drunk or just sad or what the fuck was up with you." He chuckled.

As my cheeks began to warm, I'm sure I blushed at his words.

"I'm sorry." I laughed. "And no, I wasn't drunk."

"Then what were you?" His tone was serious and all signs of a smirk were completely gone.

I couldn't find an answer for a long while as I racked my brain about what happened last night. The room fell silent and neither of us moved even the slightest. It was weird, I remembered everything from last night except how I ended up here at Colton's house...in Colton's bed.

That part made no sense at all.

I stared up at the ceiling and began to think about everything that went on last night. Isaiah's reaction still stung like an open wound but I couldn't truly blame anyone but myself.

Everyone warned me, even his own brother in a weird way. Colton told me I was being stupid and reckless but I didn't listen.

"So since you crashed at my house last night, wanna share what went on or are you gonna leave me in the dark?" Colton asked.

"Are you gonna say I told you so?" I whispered.

"Never." He replied in the same tone as before.

"Then just listen." I said while adjusting to look him in the eye.

Last Night

I brushed my hair over to the side as I stared at my reflection. My eyes held a weary look to them and I looked pale to say the least. I knew I should probably put on make up or Isaiah would instantly know something was wrong with me.

We were supposed to be going on a date today, somewhere special, he wouldn't say over the phone for some reason. I don't know if it was a surprised or if this was one of the things to knew not to announce over the phone because you know, he's been in my position before I thought bitterly.

All night I couldn't think about anything other than the information his brother had shared with me. And the fact he had a brother in the first place.

Here I was thinking I knew Isaiah so well and it's turning out I don't know him at all. How could I not know he had siblings? Why not tell someone something that simple?

Needless to say, my trust in him was beginning to perish. I wasn't sure he could do much about it either.

As I spread make up over my face, fixed my hair, and slipped into a simple blue dress all I could think about was how he was going to explain himself when I told him all I knew.

Climbing into my car and letting the music drown out my thoughts as I drove to our meeting spot, going to go see him started to seem like a really bad idea every second that went by.

Truly he couldn't fix this this time. I couldn't think of anything he could say that would make me feel better and trust him again.

A faint tap sounded from my window, snapping me out of my thoughts. I put on my best smile and rolled my window down.

"Is that how we greet each other now?" He joked. "Not even getting out the car, just rolling the window down like I'm some hooker you're meeting in a dark alley." Isaiah began laughing at his own joke.

I tried my best to chuckle along with him as I moved to get out of my car.

Once out of the car, he went for a hug and I felt my whole body freeze in place.

It wasn't supposed to be this awkward, I knew how to play happy so why couldn't I do it right now?

I felt his arms stiffen around me as he noticed I wasn't exactly hugging him back.

"What's the problem?" He asked, taking a deep breath.

What was the problem?

"No problem, I'm just tired that's all." I lied.

Isaiah placed both of his hands on either side of my face, smiling down at me. "You could've just said you were tired Stac. We could've went out tomorrow or something."

I took a deep breath, "No, I would've been tired then too."

His hands dropped from my face, his smiling slowly disappearing as he noticed I wasn't here to make jokes and laugh like we usually do.

"Was it the lady from the bathroom?" I said as his expression turned confused.

"What are you talking about?" He ran his hands through his hair, taking a deep breath.

"I meet your brother. Well more of he meet me." I began to explain while Isaiah opened his mouth to say something but I held my hand up, cutting off any sentence he had. "He told me about how you used to date your teacher." My voice was soft but I'm sure by the way he took several more deep breaths, he heard every word I said.

"Sounds like some shit he'd do." He huffed under his breath. "You have to let me explain, he probably made it sound way worse than what it actually was." He said pleadingly.

"Actually, he didn't explain the situation to me at all. What I told you is what he told me." I started, leaning against my car carelessly. "The problem is, you never even bothered to tell me any of this at all, or that you even had a brother in the first place."

Isaiah didn't speak for a long while, he only joined me against my car and stared out into space. From his expression he seemed to be in deep thought.

I was keeping my cool for the most part but my patience was beginning to dwindle. I couldn't shake the feeling that he was preparing himself to lie to me.

"Spit it out." I hissed.

His eyes met mine, his face giving off an unreadable countenance. I didn't know what to say and he probably didn't either.

"I was in college."

"Go on." I urged, crossing my arms over my chest.

"Lillian was my mentor, not necessarily my teacher." Brushing his hands through his hair and adjusting his glasses. "One day I couldn't find any inspiration for a painting so I called her and she came over to my apartment to do her job, help me. When she arrived to my apartment, it was clear she had something other than helping me in mind. She insisted on me painting her nude, it was art so I didn't think much of it. And hell, I was nineteen at the time, she was twenty-five, I was young and dumb. I wasn't going to turn down an older woman, especially one that was attractive and my teacher. That was every guy's dream."

I stared up at Isaiah as he told me what happened, he looked blankly inscrutable. I didn't speak or interupt regardless of the questions I had, I just let him go on at his own pace.

"Needless to say, me painting her nude only lasted for about two minutes and me not even touching a paint brush. Before I knew it we were kissing and all that other stuff I don't think I need to say out loud to you. Our relationship was never more than sex, we never really went out." He finished.

I nodded my head but didn't speak. I was mentally putting pieces together and something just didn't seem to add up.

"Why didn't you tell me you had a brother?" I asked after a couple minutes of silence between the two of us.

"That's another story for another day." He bit quickly.

His snappiness didn't surprise me. It was obvious his brother was another subject and clearly he didn't feel like sharing that piece today.

I racked my brain over and over again, and something was just missing. The look in his eyes when he told me about Lillian. The way he wouldn't look at me now, only slightly pass me to make it appear he was looking. It was all strange behavior for someone who really wasn't in trouble. I was just pissed I had to find out the way I did.

Still something was missing and Isaiah just looked guilty. We shared more silence and the air felt thick even though we were outside.

It hit me almost instantaneously.

"You left out something Isaiah." I laughed almost bitterly. "You've never stopped sleeping with her." I whispered.

I saw Isaiah stiffen out my peripheral vision and my eyes began to water. I knew it was all too good to be true. Here I was feeling bad about even smiling at Colton and Isaiah had never even stopped sleeping with his fucking art "mentor".

I didn't wait for him to explain, I couldn't wait for him to say anything. I wouldn't allow him to see me cry. Hell, I don't even know why I'm crying, I was basically cheating too.

I couldn't help but be hurt. Isaiah had never told me the truth. Our whole relationship has been a lie.

I yanked my car door open, starting my car and speeding off before Isaiah could even move off my vehicle.

I heard Isaiah calling my name in the distance but I didn't turn around or spare a glance. Allowing the tears to touch my cheeks, I drove and drove.

"I don't remember anything between the time I drove away from him and waking up here." I finished telling Colton about last night, taking a deep breath.

His face fell when he looked into my eyes and his only reply to my story was a big hug and in that moment, it was all I really wanted.

Chapter 25

"Liz, would you mind handing me the remote?" I stretched my arm out, putting a strained expression on my face to make it look like I was actually trying.

Liz sat on the other couch rolling her eyes because truth be told, I was closer to the remote. Although Colton did his best to cheer me up, I needed a girl. You know, a female that could understand my pain. Problem is, Liz knew nothing about Isaiah and I.

Hesitant on telling her, I called her over for a sleepover. Liz knew when something was wrong with me but surprisingly, she hadn't said a word about the fake smile I'd painted on my face when she arrived.

"You've been sitting in that same spot since I got here, just staring at the television, now you want that remote?" Liz puffed, waving her hands in the air dramatically. "I'm not getting up."

For once this whole week, I really smiled. It was weak but a smile nevertheless. It was nice to see that Liz hadn't changed since getting with Carter. Her and I weren't spending much time together these days, she's been spending most of her free time with him and skipping a few classes if they missed each other enough.

Liz began to tell me about her and Carter's new found relationship. She told me about how they went to the mall together and he actually puts up with her long visits to the dressing rooms. Things her and I used to do together.

I shook off the feeling that I was losing my best friend to my close friend and I had been allowing it to happen because I was took far up my own ass to realize it.

"There you go staring off into galaxy again." She bit out. "Are you even listening to me?"

I chuckled, "Do you mean space, Liz?"

"Whatever." She replied, throwing her hand up dismissively.

A few hours went by pf pointless conversations and best friend bickering. She mostly just went on and on about Carter. I just calmly listened and tried to remember the days where Carter was my friend as well.

He and I hadn't talked in forever. That was probably my fault too. I'd been so caught up in my own mess that I'd just been overlooking Carter completely.

"Are you even listening to me?" Liz puffed annoyed.

"Sure, I'm listening Liz." I lied.

"What's the last thing I said?" She asked, crossing her arms over her chest childishly.

"Something about Carter." I smiled sheepishly.

"I said," She emphasized, "we almost had sex."

The statement caught my attention immediately, my eyes grew big as I took in what exactly she said.

"But we're virgins." I started. "That's like our thing."

"And I still am. Hence me saying ALMOST Stac." She smiled, "I knew you weren't listening."

"Well, I am now." I crossed my legs Indian style and listened attentively to Liz tell me about the night her and Carter almost had sex.

"I was so scared, especially when his mom knocked on the door asking to speak with him. I know if she wouldn't of knocked you'd be alone in virgin world." Liz joked.

His mom? A ping of emotions ran through me, his mom had come back? For good? Carter didn't even want to step foot in the house when he thought he seen her car in his driveway, now Liz had met her? I really had been too far up my own ass lately.

I can't imagine Carter not wanting to talk about his mom. But I guess he had Liz for that now. I couldn't help but feel replaced almost. I know Liz is his girlfriend but he only knows her because of me and now I feel like I no longer know anything about him or her.

There was a time that Liz would've called me with Carter still in the room to tell me she'd almost lost her virginity. These days, she hadn't even spared me a text saying she had so much to tell me.

And here I am being hypocritical, my feelings are bruised when I was keeping a bigger secret than Li was. I had no right.

"Liz, I have something to tell you?" I cut off her rambling. I was going to just spill, get it all out and over with.

"What's up?"

"Don't be mad at me okay?" I said softly.

"I already know you kissed Carter before, I don't mind, I know you were dru-"

"Liz, shut up." I deadpanned, "it isn't about that."

She raised her eyebrow in reply but she didn't speak again.

"Its about Isaiah."

"Mr. Smith?" She cocked her head to the side in question.

I couldn't bring myself to talk so a simple nod was my reply to her. I imagined telling her my secret so many times but I never imagined I wouldn't be able to get the words out when the time came.

"Well, spit it out then." Liz said, focusing more on her nails then the fact I was over here silently freaking out.

Guess it's better to just rip the band-aid off. "We'vebeen-dating." I say in one big rushed sentence, still seeing the confusion take over her face.

"Repeat that Stac."

Taking a deep breath, I look her into the eyes. "I said, we've been dating. Like, in a relationship." I say much slower this time.

"Oh my goodness, YOU'VE HAD SEX WITH OUR ART TEACHER!" Liz whisper-shouted.

My eyes widened at her outburst. "Jesus, no!" I correct her, looking around, checking for my dad anywhere in ear distance.

"That's what you just said Stacie." She said, the smile clear in her voice.

"You're smiling." I say more to myself then her. "That's not the reaction I expected. And no, I didn't say that, I said we've been dating. Not having sex." I blushed.

"Poo, what are you waiting for. He's hot." She half joked, pouting and brushing her hands through her brown hair.

"Well, it's really a long story." I start, telling Liz all she's missed these past few months and all I've kept from her. Liz listens with minimal comments or outburst.

"I'm mad at you." She huffed, crossing her arms over her chest and putting on a childish pout.

I chuckle softly at her childlike actions but telling Liz everything only reminds me of how much Isaiah has actually lied to me. And maybe I'm overreacting but I can't help feeling like I have some right to be hurt.

"Stac, I'm just joking. You don't have to look so sad, I'm not really mad." Liz said, serious for the first time this whole night. "Hey, that rhymed!" She giggles.

I shot her a blank look, quickly wiping the silly smile off her face.

"It's really not that bad," Liz started cautiously. "He may have kept it from you because he didn't want it to play a role in your guys relationship. Besides, driving off before he could confirm or deny that he never stop sleeping with her was kind of childish Stac." She finished.

I didn't reply, only shot her another evil look.

"I mean I understand why you couldn't take it." She smiled slightly, cleaning up her last statement a little.

"It's fine Liz, I know what you meant." My voice was low, lost in my thoughts, I didn't really care what Liz was saying to me.

She made sense but I didn't want to hear rational thoughts right now, I wanted her to just be my best friend.

Tell me I was stupid for ever dating him after I found out he would be my teacher. Tell me I should just go out with Colton, make things simple for myself. Something useful, not things I already knew.

I kind of just wanted her to make my decisions for me if I'm honest. I was torn. Torn between someone I knew wasn't truly right for me and someone who I've only known for such a short time but he's done nothing but make me feel like we've been friends forever.

Colton was everything an eighteen year old would love to be in a relationship with. He was attractive, sweet, mature, caring, and just so many other things. But Isaiah, he was witty, a breath of fresh air, someone who knew who he was, someone with so much experience, someone that's just made me smile.

However, Isaiah was a liar and that one fact I couldn't shake. True, he probably had his reasons for keeping things from me but some things you should tell someone before someone else has a chance to. This was one of those things, and he failed to do that. He failed to tell me a lot. The guy I thought I knew, I didn't really know at all.

I knew the Mr.Smith that took me out on dates away from everyone. I knew the Mr.Smith that took joy in his art and knew he was talented. I knew the Mr.Smith that kissed me like we were the only two in the world. The guy that allowed me to get comfortable with the idea of us even though we truthfully stood no chance. A guy who didn't care about how dangerous our relationship really was because we liked each other that much. I knew Isaiah.

Or at least I thought I did.

I felt the couch lower under Liz's weight, her arms wrapped around me in a tight embrace and I felt tears on my face for the first time.

"It'll all work out sweetheart." I heard Liz say while she ran her hand over my hair soothingly.

I'm not sure how long I sat in my best friend's arms and cried but I knew I needed this. I needed to tell someone how I felt or least admit to myself my feelings.

I liked Colton. I liked Isaiah. Maybe not for the same reasons but the feelings were all there. And even though the choice should be obvious to me, I couldn't just pick Colton. Even after all this, I still liked Isaiah and there wasn't anything I could do to change that.

I fell asleep on the couch, wrapped up in a small ball with my head on my best friend's lap which I'm sure was uncomfortable for her but she didn't complain. She just let me sleep. She let me do what I needed. Being a better friend to me than I had been to her in a long time.

I had to go meet Carter, mom problems. Luv ya, call me if you need to talk.

I woke up with my face planted on the couch and a text from Liz. I wasn't mad she left without a goodbye, she'd given me enough of her attention for the day.

I'm sure it was now night time, there was no sun shining through the living room windows or any sign of my dad.

I pushed my body off of the couch lazily, groaning as I felt and heard my back crack at my movements.

"I wondered when you were gonna finally wake up." A voice came from the chair sitting closer to the television.

"Hi, Colton." I mumbled. My heart picked up speed as I felt my hands become sweaty.

"Hey, Stac." He replied, smiling slightly.

"Want to tell me why you're in my house and how the hell you even got in." I grumbled, sleep still clear in my voice and I'm sure I looked like crap.

"Your dad let me in on his way out and I'm here to see you." Colton said smugly. "Obviously."

"Remind me to tell dad about letting guys in to watch me sleep." I retorted sarcastically, giving Colton a tight smile.

"Will do. Now up." Was his only reply before prying my body fully off the couch and into his arms.

The simple movements from him completely woke me up. His eyes glinted from the small cast of moonlight and he seriously looked edible.

His hair was oddly neater than usual but you could tell he'd ran his hands through it a few times since arriving to my home. His chest was covered in a dark purple, cotton shirt and he had on grey sweatpants.

I couldn't tear my eyes away from his, one could say we were having a moment. Or at least, I was having a moment. A moment that ended all too soon as his hands unwrapped from around my waist and I no longer felt the heat from his effortless embrace.

Clearing my throat, I spoke softly. "What time is it?"

"Just after nine pm." He said. If going by the look on his face, he was just as shaken up as I was. He'd felt it.

I don't know if my heart should be doing flips at the fact he'd experienced that moment with me or if my brain should be telling my feet to run by now because guys just didn't seem to be working out that well for me right now.

I nodded my head in reply, turning around to lead us to my room. After reaching our destination, I pointed towards my bed silently telling him to seat there.

"I'm just gonna go get out these clothes really quick." I stated, disappearing into my closet before he could reply.

Ripping off my tank top, I slipped into an oversized sweater. Taking off my sweatpants, I decided the sweater was large enough to cover of my legs.

"So what do you want?" I shouted to Colton from inside my closet.

"I was just coming over to talk abo-" His words faded as I stepped into the main area of my room. His baby blue eyes raked over my body and I felt heat hush to my cheeks.

Not putting on any bottoms probably wasn't a good idea, for both of our sanity.

Pushing away my girly feelings, I went to join him on the bed. "About what?"

"Huh?" Question filled his face while his main focus was still my bare legs.

"Colton, up here." I laughed at his sudden distraction, happy with the results I was having on him because it really wasn't my intention to surprise him.

"If you're uncomfortable with me not having on bottoms I could always go slip something on." I began to climb off the bed again before his arm enclosed around my wrist.

"That won't be necessary." His voice was husky so he attempted to cough casually.

"Okay, so what's up." I blushed as I settled into a comfortable position on my bed without showing Colton too much.

"I came over to talk about your break up with Mr.Smith." Colton said, my eyebrows shooting up with interest. "You know, just to see if you were doing any better." He rubbed his neck nervously.

It was cute seeing Colton all red and nervous but I couldn't help but feel a little ping at my heart every time something made me think about Isaiah.

"I'm fine." I half lied. I was fine but conflicted to say the least.

"No you aren't." He whispered. "You just don't want to talk about it, and that I understand." His face broke out into a tiny grin.

I smiled at him understanding my reasons for not wanting to talk about it. My eyes ran over his stretched out figure, his arms were behind his head in a laid back position with his head placed on my pillows.

I snuggled up to Colton, taking a deep breath as I realized this felt normal. Being close to him, his warmth, it was comforting.

His hand came under my chin, lifting my head so I could look into his eyes. It felt like time slowed down as his head started to lean forward, closing the small amount of space between us.

"Colton, we probably shouldn't" I whispered.

My body was screaming at my mind to just shut up. Everything in me chanted, let him kiss you, let him kiss you.

As my eyes fluttered closed, my mouth still let words spill out. "Seriously, we probably shouldn't do this."

"You can't tell me you don't want to." Colton's voice was low, his hand still holding my chin in place.

I mumbled an incoherent response before his lips finally touched mine. My whole body lit up and my mind exploded with protest but I couldn't control myself.

The kiss was gentle so before I knew it, his lips were gone. Opening my eyes to stare up at his, my cheeks became flushed at the sight of his red lips and satisfied expression.

"He wasn't any good for you Stac." He said.

I took in his words as I shuffled back into my cozy position at his side. With my head on his shoulder, I whispered, "I have a feeling you aren't going to be either."

Chapter 26

"**O**kay class, I want you all to just freestyle today. I'm not giving you anything special to do, go with your heart. Draw, paint, sculpt, do whatever your heart feels." I listened to Isaiah's instructions but I kept my head down, making sure not to look directly at him.

The weekend had come and gone quicker than I liked and here I was sitting in class, torturing myself while Isaiah looked fine. Teaching calmly like our fight hadn't happened. Like we hadn't just decided to go separate ways.

When Isaiah was done giving instructions, he took a seat at his desk, not saying anything else to the class. I dared to lift my head only to have my eyes drawn to his that were already staring at me. I could see pleading in his eyes but the rest of his face held his calm facade.

I tore my eyes away from him. He wasn't going to make me feel guilty for leaving him like I did when I was the one that had been lied to. What am I saying? He only looked at me. I'm going crazy, reading into simple looks.

"Stacie, focus." Liz said, nudging me in the stomach.

"Stop freaking doing that!" I whispered to her while rubbing my side. "That shit really hurts." I added.

Liz's face was painted with a guilt-ridden smile, "Sorry."

We both started our art projects for the day, her humming quietly and me just doing any random lines and shapes while hoping this class went by in light speed.

Why would I get involved with my teacher? I knew we'd have to break up eventually, we never stood a chance. He was my teacher for cry-sake. I put myself through this torture knowingly and now I was sitting here pouting because I can't stand to be in the same room with him for this long.

It felt like the room was a small linen closet and Isaiah was ten times bigger than his actual size and we were the only two stuck in this sorry excuse of a closet while I was claustrophobic.

My air was running low and he felt extremely too close for me to feel any comfort. I wanted to kiss him. I wanted him to tell me everything I assumed was wrong and he was never sleeping with Lillian, the whore mentor.

The bell rang loudly over all of us students, snapping me out of my weird coping trance. The rest of the students scrabbling around putting away art supplies they were using, Liz was packing up her bag while completely ignoring her horrible art project and I myself was staring at the art project in front of me.

The sketching pencil barely had any graphite left and the paper in front me was covered with words and a girl sitting under a dead tree. I snatched up the drawing, shoving it into my bag before anyone could see what I drew.

"Stacie." I heard my name roll of his lips so I shook my head in a failed attempt of telling him not now.

"Just give me a zero for today." I muttered, gathering the rest of my things.

Liz was nowhere in sight but few students were still in the classroom so I knew Isaiah wasn't dumb enough to try anything reckless but I still felt like his presence was too close.

"I'm not giving you a zero when I watched you draw all class period." Isaiah's voice neared, busying myself with packing up more of my things.

"I said I didn't draw anything today, Mr.Smith. Have a nice day." I spoke with my head high after I finally found enough courage to look him in the eye.

Shock flashed in his eyes as I walked away without looking back or looking at the students who were giving me weird looks. I ignored them all, floating through the halls to my next class. Further away from Isaiah so I could breathe properly and try to forget the display of crazy I'd just given anyone around me back there.

I don't know why he had this affect on me but I knew I couldn't take this for the rest of the week. I'd already missed so much school, it was starting to feel like I was never here to begin with. So not coming for the rest of the week simply wasn't an option.

"Hey, Stac." Colton said before his lips rested on my own in a soft peck.

I blinked, looking at Colton with a surprised expression. "Um, Hi Colton." I greeted him back as I settled into my seat in English class.

Colton took the seat next to me, smiling like a young boy. "Sorry, that was properly strange. I should of asked first."

I nodded my head, "You should have." I smiled. "But it's fine, I don't mind kissing you."

I saw him grin happily out my peripheral vision, knowing a small smile most likely spread across my face as well.

Enlgish class went on like normal. I tuned out the teacher as I was still trying to figure out what I was doing here. On one hand I had Colton who was quickly starting to act like we were an item and on the other hand I had Isaiah who obviously had something to say to me but I didn't give him a chance.

The rest of the school day went by uneventful but I couldn't shake the haunting feeling that I needed to pick between them and pick soon.

I shoved books I didn't need into my locker while hands wrapped around my waist. I didn't jump or move out his embrace.

"Hey, Carter." I smiled, turning around and wrapping my arms around his neck in a tight hug.

"Hey, Stacie." He greeted with head resting on mine as we were still hugging.

"If I didn't know any better, I'd think you were trying to take my boyfriend." Liz cut in, winking at me.

I giggled, finally letting Carter out of our tight hug, smiling at them both.

"What's going on? Want to hang out with us?" Carter asked me, shutting my locker to get my full attention.

Still the same annoying ass he's always been I thought. "Hang out with you two? I miss you Carter but I know my best friend, she gets a little touchy. Don't want to watch you two make out and grope each other secret parts." I joked halfheartedly.

Liz threw her hands up in defense, "I do not!" She shouted with a twinkle in her eyes. "But I promise you won't have to deal with any of that today. I'm mad at him." She huffed, glaring at Carter before turning back to me and smiling.

"Ohh, relationship drama, really keeping my distance now." I laughed before another set of arms wrapped around my waist yet again.

"Well, it looks like you two finally got cozy. Liz, you owe me five dollars." Carter said.

Confusion spread across my face which I'm sure Colton's face held the same expression.

Liz groaned, pulling out five bucks and slapping it in Carter's waiting hand.

"We bet on how long it would take for you two to get together, I said a few weeks, Liz here said two months." Carter smiled triumphantly, shoving the money in his back pocket.

"Happy to know you had faith in me man." Colton said, fist pumping Carter while laughing. The two had become friends over the short time we'd all known each other.

I shook my head at all my friends, happy to finally have a normal part of my day.

"Anyway, no to hanging out with you two." I said unwrapping Colton's arms from my waist. "He and I aren't anything for now if anyone should know." I grabbed Colton's hand, lacing his fingers with my own. "See you two tomorrow, Liz text me. Carter keep in touch more often. Colton you're coming with me." I turned away from them, dragging Colton with me.

Getting in my car, I texted Isaiah to meet me at our place after telling Colton to follow behind me in his own car.

I was going to handle this once and for all and hopefully I'd leave with at least having one of them on my side.

Chapter 27

I drove quickly because Colton wouldn't stop asking a million and one questions about where I was taking him and why I was being so quiet.

What was I supposed to tell him? I'm dragging you to me and our schools art teacher secret place? No, so I kept my mouth shut, muttering a few words every once in a while so it didn't seem too strange.

I was dying inside. What if neither of them wanted to be with me? I was putting them into an awkward position and I was putting my feelings on the line.

"Still not going to tell me where you're taking me or is this some kind of weird audition you're doing for a new top secret fast and furious?" Colton tried to joke around but the confusion was evident in his voice.

I ignored his jokes, mostly because I couldn't find my voice to joke around with him. Isaiah didn't even know that any of my friends knew about us, let alone all of them. I was sure Liz had told Carter or at least I expected she would.

I pulled into our secret spot, turning off my car and still completely ignoring Colton's now annoyed questions. How would he take me confronting him? Especially with Colton here with me. I was beginning to regret my decision of dragging them both here.

It was too soon, I didn't want to lose either of them but I had a funny feeling this little meeting wasn't going to go in my favor.

Just as I went to reach for my car keys with all intention of making a B-line out of this random field not far from town, Isaiah's car drove up the small pathway blocking me inside.

I couldn't turn back now, I took a deep breath as I finally allowed myself to look in Colton's direction. You could see him connecting the dots in his head as his eyes told all. I felt all the blood drain from my face, I was now positive this was a horrible idea.

Isaiah's car turned off and his door shut quickly. I didn't give him a chance to come to my car as I climbed out of my own vehicle, knowing Colton would follow my lead.

My eyes meet with Isaiah's but his swiftly left mine the second he noticed Colton's presence as well. What I would give to know whatever he's thinking at this very moment. His expression became guarded and his eyes now mimicked Colton's cold stare while they both waited for me to announce what the hell was going on here.

"I have something to tell both of you." I started, my voice low but steady.

In unison, they nodded their heads so I continued.

"Colton, I like you." There I said it, admitted out loud for the first time since I knew. "I'm not sure when I started to or when I finally accepted it because it all just fades together. You've been here for me, kept your opinions to yourself and was just the friend I needed. I don't know if that's why I like you but you're a great guy and I feel like I've been really unfair to you."

My hands felt sweaty while I spoke some of my peace with Colton but I couldn't ignore the slight smirk on his face which I'm not sure if it was because my confession or because Isaiah's obvious tense shoulders when I spoke.

"But," I began again. "Isaiah, I like you too." Isaiah's face morphed into understanding of what was going on here, however his shoulders didn't come down from their tense position.

I stood between the two of them, my heart clenching at the realization I truly couldn't take this back now.

"Isaiah, I was hard on you, I'll say that. But you lied to me. About what, I'm still not fully aware." His mouth opened but I held my hand up to silence whatever he had to say. "I don't care, I've been unfair to you as well. I stormed away from you because my feelings were hurt, when truthfully, I don't know when was the last time I thought about just you. He-" I pointed towards Colton, "has been on my mind as well since the day I found out he was moving in next door to me."

Isaiah's face no longer held any expression, it was as though he was just taking in my words.

"So." I spoke to both of them. "I know this sounds bad but I just figured I should be truthful with both of you. At least now, before I get deeper in to anything with both of you."

I didn't expect them to just pull me into long hugs and tell me they weren't going anywhere after what I'd just confessed. I just hoped somebody would say something soon because my mind was racing and the silence around us was too thick for anyone to be comfortable.

"I lied to you." He spoke up.

Isaiah.

"I strung you along when I knew pieces of my past weren't all just behind me. But Stac," Isaiah came forward, closing some of the distance between us two. His fingers twitched but he still didn't touch me. "It's really not what you think. I should of told you about Lillian before anyone else had a chance to. Honestly, I was in no rush to tell you about my past because I thought no one could beat me to it. The idea of us is crazy, but if I haven't said it before, I'll say it now." His eyes flickered over to quiet Colton before returning back to mine, his own overflowing with emotions.

"I love you. Dammit, I said it. And I've known since the day I watched you walk away from me, shattered because of me. I love you, I'll shout it to the world if I have to. We're crazy. Us, it's crazy. But I'll do whatever I need to you to get a true chance with you." He finished.

The world had slowed down and for the quickest second, Colton didn't matter to me. He'd said it. Not only to me but in front of someone else. His eyes shined with truth but deep down I still felt guarded.

"But I see, you have something or someone in the way for you to feel the same." Isaiah whispered, his hands cupped my cheeks. "And I'll allow you to figure that out before I ask you to properly be with me." Placing a soft kiss on my forehead, Isaiah tucked his hands into his jean pockets and created space between us once more.

What was I supposed to say? I wasn't sure if I even understood what he was offering me. Was it true? Would he step down from his job to allow us a real chance with each other or was I assuming that's what he meant. Love or not, he and I stood no chance without a lawsuit and chaos coming soon behind.

"Stacie." Colton's voice pulling me out of my confused stare.

I nodded in response, not trusting my voice enough to speak out to him.

"I don't love you." My eyes snapped up in his direction, his face full of determination. "But I could grow to. We, together, could work towards that. Build and let ourselves fall and I promise, I'll always be here to catch you." A small smile tugging at his lips as he took steps towards me.

"I like you. I like your spirit. The way you smile to yourself in your room when you're drawing all alone. I like how your face screams all your thoughts and every time we're together a good time is effortless. But I won't compete for your love. I won't tell you to pick me or point out all his flaws. I'll let you decide because Stac, you deserve that much." Colton's voice held no secrets as he spoke his side.

Wrapping his arm around my waist, gently dragging my body to his as if he and I were the only two in this field. I didn't fight or pull away from his hold while I watched him lean down cautiously.

His lips only inches from mine, he moved at a deathly slow pace as if silently asking for permission. My eyes fluttered closed, our faces so close I felt my eye lashes brush across his cheeks.

Colton took my silence as acceptance, diminishing the little space between my lips and his own. A soft, faint kiss it was but it held so much emotion that I couldn't pull away even if I wanted to.

This wasn't how I expected any of this to go. They didn't hate me? Call me mean names because I had strung them both along with my indecision. No, they were both giving me a chance to choose. They weren't leaving me alone with neither as an option. Much to my surprised, they'd both basically just promised to stick around as long as I wanted them to.

I no longer felt his lips or his arm around my waist at that moment while I crawled back out of my thoughts.

Both guys stood next to each other both looking at me like the balls were now in my court.

"We aren't asking you to choose now." Isaiah started.

"Or even right away." Colton said.

"Take your time." Isaiah rocked back and forth on his toes, a nervous thing I'd seen him do so many times before.

"I'm not going anywhere." Colton whispered, loud enough for both Isaiah and myself to hear.

"We'll give you time. Colton, would you like a lift?" Isaiah offered, no longer paying attention to me or the fact that I stood here at a lost for words.

Colton nodded, "Thanks. I'll see you around Stac."

They two turned away from me, heading back to Isaiah's car. No one said another word and I couldn't believe what had just happened around me.

I watched the two pull away from the quiet field and I felt myself finally breathe. They were going to let me choose. They were really going to let me choose.

My heart stopped at the realization that no matter how much both promised they weren't going anywhere, I couldn't have both of them.

Chapter 28

Two weeks had went by since my little chat with the guys in the field. Neither were giving me the cold shoulder, and they both were surprisingly understanding of me still not knowing who I would choose.

I tried spending time with Isaiah and Colton equally but it was really hard not to lean more towards Colton when all my time with Isaiah was limited and usually involved a long drive so no one we knew could spot us together.

I knew the risk of picking Isaiah. His job. His reputation. My reputation and my education if it actually went that far. Our relationship would never be a walk in the park. Even if he decided to quit at the school, we'd still have to remain a secret for a little longer. That piece made me uncomfortable.

There was no true way to become public with Isaiah. We both were starting to realize that much. Our conversations half the time were stressful because neither of us knew what to do. Isaiah loves his job as much as he loves art. I couldn't really allow him to quit just to be with me.

However, it was a fairytale to believe he and I could last as a secret until I graduated next year. I mean, his brother had already found out about us, how? Who the hell knew but it obviously meant he and I didn't truly know how to hide our relationship.

From my understanding, Isaiah and his brother weren't even close anymore so if he could find out, anyone could. As exciting and thrilling as our relationship was when it first started, reality was beginning to set it. We both had too much to lose to be together right now.

But he loved me, and I somewhat loved him too. Although my feelings for Isaiah were genuine, they were clouded by my feelings for Colton as well.

Colton, we'd spent so much time together over the past two weeks people were beginning to think we were dating anyway. Understandable, because we kind of were. He lays with me and watches my favorites movies, even if he doesn't care for them. His hands always find a way to my hair when he snuggle up on one of our beds for the day while we talk for hours at a time.

Getting to know each other. Learning the in and outs of of one another. What the other liked and disliked. What made us tick and how we act when we're hungry or tired. We'd even hung around Liz and Carter a few times, something Isaiah and I currently couldn't do. They knew everything, about Isaiah and I but having us all hang together would be strange. He's their teacher too.

Little things that Colton and I could do that I didn't have the luxury of doing with Isaiah. Colton and I hung out at local dinners and coffee shops, saw movies that weren't at least two hours away, and even held hands sometimes if I didn't pull away when he laced his fingers through my own.

As I laid in my bed, lost in these thoughts, I couldn't help but feel like I didn't deserve either one. My phone kept beeping over and over again, but I decided to ignore whoever it was. I needed to get my thoughts together.

Two weeks was enough. They told me to take my time but at this point, I was only making things worth by dating both of them.

A timid knock sounded from my bedroom door, but again, I ignored them too. Figuring eventually they would just go away, I was wrong.

"Do you honestly think laying in bed all day is going to fix whatever problems you obviously are having at the moment?" Carter said from my doorway.

"Just invite yourself in. Sure, I'd love some company." I bit out with a roll of my eyes.

"I know, that's why I popped up. You're so lucky to have a great friend like me." He plastered on his signature grin, jumping onto my bed while doing so.

I pushed Carter off my leg, choosing to just sit up because he wasn't planning on moving. "I just met you this year, I don't know how great you are." I joked.

I didn't mind having company but I just wanted to be alone in my thoughts.

"I'm listening." Carter folded up his arms, laying his head on top of them like his own personal pillow as he looked up at my sitting form, waiting to hear what I had to say.

"There's nothing to listen to." I shrugged. He wouldn't get it.

"Then why did Colton text me, saying to come check up on you." Carter said after shoving his phone in my face.

My eyes narrowed as I looked at his text and my gaze quickly found its way to the window where I found a smiling Colton. His hand was rubbing his neck and his face was filled with nerves. Colton just waved and disappeared from my sight.

"If he wanted to know what was wrong with me, why not just ask instead of being a peeping tom?" I wasn't mad but I'd rolled my eyes at least five times since Carter stepped foot in my room less than three minutes ago.

"Maybe he did try to ask." His eyes were on my phone that was currently across the room, untouched.

"Can't a girl ignore her phone every once in a while?" I said, sheepishly smiling or at least trying to.

"It's okay if you're unsure you know." He started.

I nodded my head but I kept my mouth closed.

"It's a complicated situation you've allowed to go on for a really long time, Stac. I'm your friend and I'm going to be honest with you, always. You know that right?"

I nodded again, waiting for him to go on.

"Colton won't be waiting around for you forever." My heart stopped. He'd only spoke what I knew all along but did he know something I didn't? The two have grown close, maybe he'd told Carter about someone else.

The jealously that sparked inside of me was unfair but I couldn't help it. I really like the guy.

"Don't look so shaken up. There's no one else, I'm just telling you it could be. If you wait too long." Carter said in a soft voice.

"But what about Isaiah?" My voice was low, my eyes staring off into Colton's bedroom window.

"What about him?" Carter sat up suddenly. "You can't seriously be considering this dude?" I'm sure my face said it all.

"Stacie, seriously?"

I shrugged my shoulders aftering brushing loose hairs behind my ear. "We fit, Carter. He's a nice guy. You don't know him like I do."

"Stac, are you sure you even know this guy at all? I mean what's a few hook ups and a couple secret dates. Screw knowing his favorite colors and favorite foods. What else do you know?" Carter shot off aggressively, his eyes lighting up with every word.

"I know more than that!" I shot back with just as much aggression.

"What's his mom's name?"

"What's his father's name?"

"How many siblings does he have?"

"Is he allergic to any animals? Foods?"

"What does he do when he can't sleep?"

"What calms him down when he's nervous?"

Carter shot the questions at me like he was the guy I was choosing between. His face was a bright red and the frustration in his eyes and voice were all there. Still, the question threw me into a whole new realm of thinking.

I didn't know those things about Isaiah at all. But I didn't know those things because they were secrets, I didn't know those things because I never asked and with Isaiah it was don't ask, won't tell.

"See, you don't know him like you think you do." Carter's voice was calm now even though his eyes told his true opinion.

"What are you getting at, Carter?" I didn't yell but I rolled my eyes for good measure.

"I'm saying you don't know him well enough to risk everything for him. You guys relationship is impossible Stac, and you know it. We all do. I'm sure he does too. Put your attraction aside, is it really worth losing everything for? Not just you, him too, especially him. Think about it, Stac. You have a great guy living next to you, ready to get to know you better but he can't do that if someone else is getting to know you too." Carter got up and left my room before I could fully let his words sink in.

It wasn't his choice to make. It was mine.

I got up, showered and fixed my hair. Allowing it to wave which way it may, I got dressed. Simple black jeans, a tank top, and my brown boots, I put on my coat and rushed out the house.

Phone in hand, I knew what I had to do, who I had to call.

Chapter 29

The wind was harsh and my small brown trench coat was cute, but it definitely wasn't keeping me warm. My hair blew all over, it was a really bad idea to leave the house with wet hair in this weather.

I could've been sitting in my car but I couldn't find it in myself to sit still. My hands kept running up and down my jeans at their own accord and regardless of how cold it was I could feel sweat forming at my neck.

I'd sent out my texts, made my calls to be sure, all I had to do was wait. Well waiting deemed itself a harder task than I expected. Would he show up? Would I be able to go through with everything I promised myself I'd do when I finally made this decision? Would I regret my choice?

All these questions jogged through my head, a marathon of questions I couldn't answer. Time wasn't my friend. It felt like I'd been waiting for days. Days in the same spot, doing the same thing, just waiting. I didn't know how to take it.

It was like having a presentation for the first time in middle school and all you can think about is if anyone was going to pay attention or if you were going to mess up all the words you'd went over so many times in your head. You didn't want to mess up because you were presenting in front of someone you'd have to see again once it was all over.

To sum up my feelings in one word, nervous. I was nervous. Scared out of my boots because this was my life. Sure, I'm young but this choice right now made my next few months at least.

Shadows moving in my peripheral vision reluctantly pulled me out of my nervous thoughts. His hair was messy, his grey shirt longer than his thin spring jacket stood out against his dark jeans, and overall he looked tired.

Hands stuffed into the pockets of his jacket, he came to a halt in front of me. He didn't speak or reach to touch me like I was used to.

It stung, seeing him. Like this. Any other time we met outside of school it was filled with laughs and good vibes, today he looked ready to accept whatever I said before I even uttered a word to him.

He already looked hurt without me having to open my mouth.

Out of habit I pulled him into a hug. His tall build making it harder for me to wrap my arms around his neck but I needed this. I needed to be sated by his natural scent. I needed to feel some kind of comfort. I couldn't say what I had to say without it, my nerves wouldn't allow me to.

For a long while, he didn't move to hug me back. Standing unruffled by my hug, we stood that way, with my arms wrapped tightly around his neck while his arms stayed firm on my waist, not really hugging me back but granting me with some kind of contact.

I pulled back to meet hazel eyes and as cliche it sounds, it was like my world slowed down a little. Tiny specks of gold that used to live there were dark, saddened, and I felt like it was possibly my fault.

"Get on with it, Stac." He said, his voice a whisper between the small space between us.

I leaned up to press my lips against his. A small spark shooting up my spine and traveling to my arms and back as his returned my gentle kiss. We didn't move away or make the kiss deeper. Just his lips on mine and mine on his in a kiss that felt so simple but full of emotion that I wasn't really sure I understood.

"This is so stupid." I blew out once we pulled apart.

My right hand laid on his cheek as my left played with a few strands of hair that fell at the back of his neck.

"This is so silly. Me. Us. Here. It's so silly and it's so confusing and I'm so sorry for ever putting you through this." I started, while it took everything in me to continue looking into his eyes, I continued. "I was selfish. To continue stringing you along when I knew someone else partly had my attention. Rather consciously or not, I felt it. Felt something else pulling my attention but still, I selfishly clung onto both of you and for that I'm sorry."

He didn't say much, only the occasionally nod. I took it as him allowing me to speak so I went on.

"Isaiah, I'm so sorry. I shou-" I began again before his abrupt kiss silenced all my upcoming words.

The kiss much more romantic than the last. His hands met my still damp hair, pulling softly at the blonde strands. My mind got lost in our kiss while his lips sucked away any trace of bad words I had left to say. Our lips worked in sync and the kiss was mind numbing, over way too soon.

"I know it'll be our last time." Isaiah said softly while our foreheads rested on each others.

"Sadly, it will and I'm so sorry." I chuckled solemnly.

Isaiah only nodded his head and hid his eyes under his thick lashes, casting his gaze elsewhere.

"You're great. But I won't allow you to risk it. I can't risk it. It's your job. Our reputations. Your life. As much as we feel like we work, and we're great together, the law doesn't feel the same. They don't care about how much we have in common or how we truly meet. The world out there, is unforgiving. I love you too much to do that to you. I won't. But as much as I love you, I'm not in love with you, Isaiah. We've both known it for a long time I think. You aren't in love with me either.

What we had was something special, but what I can have with someone else can be just as special. And we won't have to be a secret. We won't have to worry about being seen or what people will think if they found out and I think at my age I deserve that. You deserve that, to be with someone you can show off and be shown off yourself. We're complicated and complications aren't what we both need right now." I said with a sigh.

Isaiah looked at me like I was the most complex piece of art he'd ever laid his eyes on and he smiled. "You can meet the perfect person at the worst time. That's what happened to us, Stac. When I seen you at the cafe that was my chance to start over. Get away from people like Lillian and my brother. My mistake was expecting you to be okay with sharing yourself when I didn't share any pieces of me. I kept my secrets and expected all of yours, for that I'm sorry. How I wish I wasn't your teacher, I'd probably be begging you to reconsider right now." He smiled, tucking a strand of hair behind my cold ears.

"But you're right, we are a huge risk. One I was selfish to expect you to take because I was willing to. You're stubborn, I knew that early on, I should have known you wouldn't allow us to go on long." Isaiah said while pulling me into a big hug, one I quickly returned.

All my nerves from before vanished into thin air as I hugged Isaiah tightly. A faint, relieved smile painted my face after he pulled away from me.

"You'll always be my one that got away." He kissed my forehead tenderly.

I nodded as I lifted my head from his hold to look into his soft hazel eyes this way one last time. "I just hope you understand."

We unwrapped ourselves from each others hold and Isaiah didn't speak anymore. He granted me with a slight nod before he briskly walked away.

It felt like a weight I was unaware of had been heaved off my back and my world suddenly seemed just a tad clearer. I knew who I wanted, I just hoped he still wanted me.

Epilogue

I rushed home that night and I didn't do what I told myself I was going to do. The whole drive home, I'd convinced myself to wait one more day. Allow my mind to be fully clear I guess you could say.

I didn't want Colton to feel like he was some sort of re-bound. He wasn't. I can't say it's always been him, but he's been my choice for some time.

I wouldn't allow myself to believe it because for a long time, feeling anything for Colton simply felt wrong when I knew I had Isaiah in the picture, regardless of what he and I were going through.

I had no right to feel something, chemistry, a spark, any-thing, with someone other than Isaiah. So I pushed my feel-ings to the side. Denied them. I wasn't going to do that any longer.

Witht that mindset, that's how I ended up here. Sunday morning, a full nights rest, a clear head, and for the first time in a while; fully single.

And I was hoping to change that soon. I climbed out of bed and did the normal routine. You know, brush your teeth, wash your face, shower, breakfast. I did it all, and after that I spent a hour talking myself into walking a yard over to confess my feelings.

In all honesty, I didn't want to be rejected. He had every right to do so. I'd waited so long to say something, anything. I knew if he rejected my today, it was no ones fault but my own.

My phone buzzed in the back pocket of my jeans, halting my thinking and gathering my full attention.

"I see you pacing, come over and we can talk about it."

The text read. I couldn't help but smile slightly. He had no idea he was the reason I was pacing. I looked up to see him leaning against his window, looking directly at me and waiting for my response.

Instead of replying, I gave him a thumbs up and turned my back away from the window before he could see my face flush.

This was it. It was now or never. Maybe I was being dramatic but that's what it felt like. Like what he decided after I spilled out my guts would dictate my mood for a long time. That's a lot of power to give someone, so how could I be so sure that I'm ready?

I took a few deep breaths as I left my bedroom.

"Dad, I'll be back in a few." I yelled down the hallway.

My dad had been home a lot more lately, we still didn't bond much but at least I got to see his face every once in a while.

I heard a faint okay but I was already half way out the door. The wind made the air crisp and chilly but that was normal for a winter to spring transitioning day.

My lazy sweater and jogging pants kept me warm on the walk over to Colton's home. He greeted my at the door like always and we walked to his room in silence.

His hair looked slept on and his clothes were lazy like my own. Before I knew it were inside his room just sitting on his bed with our arms crossed over our legs like it was our first time being around each other.

"It's okay to tell me. I've pretty much been over here hurting my feelings since we agreed to let you choose. I get it. He's older, he's tall. Not taller than me but whatever." Colton started with a smile.

"I understand why you don't want to-"

"Colton, I choose you." I cut him off, placing my hand over top of his.

"What?" His eyes bulged out his head as he whipped his head in my direction fast enough to break his neck.

"I said, I choose you." My voice was stronger this time, a grin spreading over my face. "I talked with him yesterday, I ended everything."

"Tell me you aren't joking." Colton said, his smile matching my own.

I shook my head fiercely. "I'm totally serious."

There was a glow that passed through his eyes that made my heart do a thousand flips and butterflies erupt in my stomach. He still wanted me.

"Colton, I'm so sorry for putting you through all of this. You didn't deserve to be in the middle of my mess. You didn't deserve me making you wait until I made up my mind. You're a good guy. I know that, I see that now. And I'm hoping you want to give this a go. But you know, we can take it slow if you want. That's fine too. I don't want to rush you into anyt-"

Colton lips smashed against mine, kissing away any trace of doubt I had that he might not really want this anymore. Our lips moved in sync in a gentle but passionate kiss that seemed to last a lifetime.

"Stacy, I'm the lucky one here." Colton said with his forehead pressed against mine, breathing slightly heavier than before.

"I have no idea what you two see in me." I huffed.

"And it doesn't matter, as long as we see something worth fighting for." Colton brushed stray strands of hair behind my ear, placing a light peck on my lips. "Let's just start over." He said.

I nodded my head in agreement. "Hi, my name is, Stacy." I pulled out of his hold and held out my hand for him to shake.

Colton stared at my hand before letting out a small chuckle. "I hate you. My name is, Colton." He shook my hand while leaning in to kiss one more time.

www.ingramcontent.com/pod-product-compliance
Lightning Source LLC
Chambersburg PA
CBHW071818190726
48292CB00005B/1507